TENNESSEE BLUE

The Future Is Not What It Used to Be

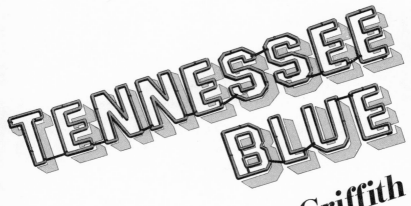

TENNESSEE BLUE

Patricia Browning Griffith

CLARKSON N. POTTER, INC. / PUBLISHERS • **NEW YORK**
Distributed by CROWN PUBLISHERS, INC.

Grateful acknowledgment is made for permission
to reprint the following:

"Gettin' By"
Used by permission. All rights reserved
by Groper Music. Copyright © 1973.

Excerpt from *The Death of Artemio Cruz* by Carlos Fuentes.
Copyright © 1964 by Carlos Fuentes.
Reprinted by permission of Farrar, Straus and Giroux, Inc.

Inquiries should be addressed to Clarkson N. Potter, Inc.,
One Park Avenue, New York, New York 10016
Printed in the United States of America
Published simultaneously in Canada
by General Publishing Company Limited
Library of Congress Cataloging in Publication Data
Griffith, Patricia Browning.
Tennessee Blue.
I. Title.
PS3557.R489T4   1981   813'.54   80-25626
ISBN: 0-517-541874
Designed by Camilla Filancia
10 9 8 7 6 5 4 3 2 1
First Edition

To my daughter Ellen Flannery

No one will really be aware except you yourself, that your existence will be woven of all the threads in the loom, exactly as are the lives of all men. There will not be lacking, nor will there be more than, one single opportunity to make your days what you want them to be. And if you become one thing rather than another, that will be because in spite of everything you will have to choose.

From *The Death of Artemio Cruz*
by CARLOS FUENTES

translated from the Spanish
by SAM HILEMAN

TENNESSEE BLUE

Being out of work for sixty-three consecutive days has led George Perry to certain conclusions: The gray federal buildings lined along the Washington Mall are the heart of the city. The heart is therefore granite, stone, marble, steelbraced, precast concrete, impenetrable. Choose one. The days and nights go by but the gray isn't altered. The night doesn't mellow, the sun doesn't lighten. They cast no shadows. Love has never touched them, lovers never entered their doorways. Arms resting on their metal desks are constantly chilled.

For six years George Perry, professional journalist of good standing reduced by the exigencies of economics and fate to government information officer, walked the shiny corridors, the new ones with color-coordinated halls that don't always connect. When he thinks of the years he thinks of himself always in motion, walking, head up, looking for a number beside the identical doors, his mind blinded on either side by the width of the corridor. The time afterwards at his typewriter he's nearly forgotten, or at least hidden from himself, expended as it was in mimeographed releases measured ultimately in column inches.

The merging of his being with the stone around him has happened gradually, slowly, so that he hasn't realized the union until the sixty-three days of unemployment during which he's recognized the coldness in his bones and known that he and the buildings have become one. Married, indeed. Nearer than anyone in the world. In death they may part but he doubts it. He will take his place, invisible along an assigned corridor, his presence felt only in the slight alteration of echo as one passes.

George Perry glances out the window where the rain has changed the chameleon-like buildings to their darkest shades while he is relatively dry and warm inside the yellow neon bubble of the Capitol Coffee Shop. The Capitol Coffee Shop, an equal opportunity purveyor of jelly, glazed and plain doughnuts to any person capable of sliding twenty cents across the yellow Formica toward Nadine the waitress who should have been at home nodding over "As the World Turns" instead of toting trays of doughnuts, her fat arms pinched circles under the short sleeves of her nylon uniform.

George takes a taste of bitter coffee and glances across the room at the young man who followed him there. He is maybe twenty and extremely thin and narrow. A big western straw hat presses on a confusion of brown hair. He bends over a blue notebook, writing, the sleeves of his denim jacket far short of his wrists. On the floor beside him a blue rectangular Leatherette case rests protectively against his legs.

The kid looks up from the writing suddenly and George looks away. When he glances again the boy is smiling at him with bright blue eyes. The face is crude, all harsh angles with no soft middle-class curves. It presents all possibilities. It makes George think of Claudie, his daughter, so he dismisses the kid, thinking maybe he's mistaken, the kid hasn't followed him there.

But the writing intrigues him, reminds him of himself once, dreaming of writing in cafes, of bullfights and mysterious and accessible girls. Of course he did write, news for thirteen years, press releases for six, but never literature, and his only arena is the small glass stage of a TV screen where the Redskins struggle, and his first beautiful woman is nearly forty and living with someone thirty-five and his conversations with her are stilted all right but not loving. And his second beautiful woman is perhaps too mysterious for him to understand.

Across from him Nadine slides a long metal tray of freshly iced doughnuts onto a shelf and he smells the fresh icing with his recently un-nicotine-clogged nose and finds the sweet smell unpleasant. He's found no advantages in being able to smell again.

Suddenly the kid closes his book and stuffs it into a

green khaki satchel. He litts the blue case onto the table, unlatches the clasp and removes the top to reveal a keyboard. He plugs the cord into a wall socket and waits a moment poised before the keys, then begins to play. The sound is loud and electric. Nadine smiles, a gold-flecked smile, as she turns from the coffee maker.

There's dancing at the FBI
Every Tuesday at ten
There's ties and spies and dragonflies
And June from outer space

His voice is shrill and unlikely. The waitress watches with her pinched arms folded. A black schoolgirl smiles suspiciously. A woman in a plastic raincoat next to George drinks her tea with weary disinterest.

June from outer space
Fell in love with an agent there
But she had to return, so he dances alone
Every Tuesday at ten

George buttons his coat and shoves a quarter next to his cup. Passing the kid he drops a quarter into the top of the case.

"June thanks you and I thank you," the kid says, playing on.

At the doorway he stops to put another coin into a slot and pulls out the afternoon paper. Its face is familiar as a wife's. He fed it for six years and scanned its every word daily looking for his own information, his own lies and propaganda. Seeing it, there is still a twinge of pain like seeing an old lover.

Outside the rain is steady. He decides not to try the new personnel consultant after all. He'd be wet by the time he got there and orderliness was of utmost importance. By now he's perfected the whole orderly technique, calmly meeting their eyes, his own testifying to sixteen years of steadiness and hygiene, sixteen years of 6:45 alarm clocks and public transport for breakfast.

When he closes the door the organ is faint and then quickly is lost as he joins the flow of shoppers, hurrying out of habit like those alongside him. In the doorway of an old building a flower seller huddles before daffodils bright as miracles in the dull rain.

It's early for those, George thinks, *but then you say that every year, don't you, George. It is spring*. He talks to himself nowadays. He has moments when he is so alone with himself that he seems turned inside out, alone inside the dark physical machinery of his ongoing life, a factory without control or exit. This feeling frightens him because he is forty-four, too young to be left alone with himself and too old for it to be such a problem. It is a dangerous thing, this self-consciousness. It leads one down wrong corridors and through wrong doors.

At a movie theatre he pushes money toward a heavy-set white woman sitting in a glassed cloud of cigarette smoke like one of those glass balls that snow when shaken. She pushes a ticket out with a hand ringed on every finger.

"Have fun," she says grimly.

The movie is a thriller laced with several old stars in cameo roles. The leads are young and hardly identifiable. The old stars look old.

It is halfway through the movie before he smells the daffodils, fresh and startling in the bland gray glow of the theatre that earlier smelled of almond disinfectant. He turns and finds the kid who played the chord organ sitting behind him, holding a bouquet.

It is dinner time in the cafeteria and the room is filled with the cautious movement of old people. When they entered the kid distributed the daffodils to several old ladies who are now giving him suspicious glances. With the chord organ beneath his feet his knees are blue nubs on the other side of the table.

"My name is Tennessee Blue," he says. "My mother made it up. Blue she liked and Tennessee she wanted to go to. My father went to Tennessee to get rich in automated car washes. Merle—that's my mother—thought she'd pretty soon be honeymooning in Las Vegas and playing the money machines but she never heard from him again." Tennessee stirs his orange drink with his straw.

"Where's home?" George asks, feeling nearly disarmed of suspicion by the kid's openness.

"Mostly West Virginia," Tennessee says, his eyes blue

as Bic pen tops. He came to D.C. when he was twelve, he tells George, not telling him all of it, him and Merle living for a week in a car off East Capitol extended, eating out of vending machines in a laundromat and service station. Sitting there for most of a week looking at a sign FOR SALE, ZONED COMMERCIAL and "Christmas Trees Here" though it was February and the Christmas tree was one nude pine weathering into the ground. And Merle crying and drinking and praying until the service station attendant called the cops. And the cop gliding easy across the highway on his Harley-Davidson and his mother still sleeping with newspapers on the windows blocking the sun. He shook her awake and she rose, pushing on her yellow hair, rolling down the window, saying, "Morning!" to the cop like she was rising from her bed back in West Virginia.

"You got car trouble?" the cop said.

"I tell you officer, I got one Jesus lovin' more'n car trouble!" Then telling him most of it, not all, about coming from West Virginia nine days ago and the car breaking down and the man running out and leaving her and the boy and no money to speak of and her not knowing one holy soul in that town and being scared, scared, ever' minute praying to the Lord for the safety of herself and her son and hoping the man would get his senses and come back. And she would sure appreciate some assistance.

The cop made a phone call and in a while a patrol car came for them. His mother called, *"God bless you a lot, officer,"* and Tennessee knew from watching the cop's face that he'd see him again. And he did a few times after they left the emergency shelter until the other man returned for a while, long enough to move them elsewhere, down into Virginia . . .

"I've moved around a lot—San Francisco, L.A., Austin. I write songs." He says it with importance as though he'd said, *"I build bombs."*

"And what brings you back to D.C.?" George asks.

"Friends," Tennessee says, "and business." He tells George there's lots of music around D.C. and he writes songs for a rock band called Lost in Space. Lost in Space, he says, is really into space—the Invisible College, Project Starlight International, all that. They figure there'll be positive proof of extraterrestrial travel before long. The government probably has it already. "Don't you think?" he asks George watching him intently.

"I never thought about it," George says, knowing that if he were to think about it, the subject would sift through, dismissed without thought.

"Nowadays, you know, people turn to space like they used to turn to religion. They have a lot in common. The Bible has space travel. Especially the book of Revelation. Talks about 'a rainbow like unto an emerald.' That's nice, isn't it? Sounds like music."

George shrugs uncomfortably thinking of his own unextraordinary interests—a job, one woman and a desire to lay the ghosts. Surely little enough for one man to handle.

At the next table a very old man with a hearing aid on each ear is laughing loudly with three ladies and George, feeling Tennessee studying him, wants to escape Tennessee and the old people and the stuffy cafeteria smelling of steamed food.

He finishes his coffee and rises. "Well, good luck, Tennessee," he says, wanting to laugh at the name.

"See ya around," Tennessee calls, and George thinks, I hope not, as he makes his way through the tables of old people. At the door he glances back to see Tennessee looking after him, strange and smiling to himself.

It is nearly dark outside, the rain lighter, the traffic slow. The government workers have departed their hill for the night leaving the city people behind. It is like the end of a party every evening with only best friends and drunks remaining.

He walks a half-block to the bus stop. He could walk home across Lafayette Park and up Connecticut. He'd be home in twenty minutes. But it is raining slightly and he would miss the bus conversations and the varied faces that he enjoys in the brief minutes with the typical bizarre bus community. Deep down he is a gregarious person in an ungregarious place and time. Elizabeth says that. Elizabeth is always right. He should be in some friendly village with town meetings and community sings and Homecoming queens. Anywhere but in this political city where the political wheel paddles steadily, its own city perimeters hit the hardest with each revolution while elsewhere across the land the water is only slightly stirred.

His bus appears and George steps forward but the driver's face never turns and the bus passes, rushing through the changing light leaving its fumes. He curses after the half-empty bus and walks up the street to a bar, orders a drink and leans on a rail where Lincoln is said to have leaned. On a ledge is a baseball autographed by Babe Ruth. It is a city of relics in a country uneasy with relics. When he leaves it is night and he begins walking. Ahead the lights of the bars and porno houses on 14th Street glitter cleanly in the light rain. The block was once a happy combination of beer parlors, night clubs and strip joints. Now it's all hard stuff—porno bookstores and taverns with porn movies, not even live people. The real people are out on the streets in tall heeled boots and body-hugging skirts while dudes in sweeping hats inside their shiny late-model hogs share vigilance with two policemen and a dog. It is only three blocks to the White House but another world. He likes Washington for that, for the proximity of powers. Bargains of sex negotiated on one corner while three blocks away negotiations of another kind of force are carried on.

He crosses against the light at the corner partially closed for subway construction. There beneath the street for blocks lies a great dark cavern of raw earth covered with slick boards that occasionally give slightly under his weight. Across the street he glances back and sees a tall, slender figure a block behind, following. Then he sees the alleyway ahead and some moment of premonition that prepares for both magic and death touches him even before the arm and the blow to his head and the pulling from behind and the second blow that brings the violet light from the Star-Spangled Club down the block to wrap around his head like a misty turban before it blacks out everything except the feeling of falling down

and

down.

So how to begin? As a song writer I should pull out a long funky droopy-drawers number. A lot of blues, heavy on percussion, amplifiers turned up to Australia. The trouble with words alone is they quit too soon. And I wasn't taught to count much on the facts. Merle could talk the leaves off the trees. It comes with religion, Merle said. Imagination. Imagination grows the daisies in your mind. Facts stomp 'em out. But forget the daisies. No daisies at Ferguson. Only metal. Bars. Ferguson, a parcel of the Texas Correctional System. Over ten months of it. Like carrying a camel across a desert, a buffalo across Montana. Till finally I had serious business on the outside. So I make scratches on a paper for a furlough. They do that now in prisons. Somebody I knew got a furlough when his mother croaked from a daily dose of four packs of Pall Mall and a quart of Old Granddad. Another guy when his wife got held hostage by an Oklahoma lunatic wanting media coverage. I told them on the paper I wanted a furlough to save somebody's life. They were supposed to be into that kind of thing. But that wasn't a good enough reason for them. So I proceeded to make my own plans.

We were on the prison bus that day heading for the school house like every Monday-Wednesday-Friday. In Texas the highways are built up higher than the land. You can drive by and look down on the cons out working. We grew rice and sugarcane and broomcorn. It was April so the fields were brown and empty except for rattlesnakes and fourteen thousand kinds of stinging and biting bugs. There were twenty-one of us in the bus not counting the guard and driver and the shotgun, everybody sleeping or looking out the windows at where they knew they couldn't be. I leaned forward and called out to the guard that I didn't feel too good.

He says, "You don't look too good either. You puke in the bus you'll get your ass kicked," *he said.*

Ferguson Unit is for first offenders, 17–21. It has a mop and broom factory. They claim to emphasize educational and vocational training. What the guard says when you first get there is, "Fuck up on this school shit and your ass has had it. You'll be gettin' your balls broke in Huntsville." *So I signed up for Business Letter Writing 121, learning to be a tycoon, I said.*

About that time I did feel sick, like the metal was growing into my stomach and rusting there. When we got to

*the college we filed by the guard and I held my stomach,
indicating severe pain and suffering and he says, "Tough
shit," real sympathetically.*

*Instead of going to the classroom I went to the john
knowing they wouldn't report me right off since I was sick.
Inside the john some guy was smoking grass. The month
before a friend of mine claimed he made it in there with a
girl from Conversational Spanish. Anyway, I went right to
the window and pushed open the metal grating that'd
already been broken away. The guard was in front with the
bus. All he had to do was look up and he could see me
dropping out the window but sometimes he talked to the
driver or read the sports page of the* Huntsville Item *or went
inside for coffee or had a nip with the driver behind the bus.*

*So I tried not to think about the guard. I dropped out
the window behind a bush and slouched to the sidewalk like
any punk student instead of a six-foot-two fink-haired con
willing to helicopter to the moon to get away from there. I
rounded the building and there was the van, Warren
waiting inside with a six-pack of beer and a bushy brown
wig and Willie and Waylon singing "Good Hearted
Woman" on a cassette. I told Warren this was as good as a
movie and I tossed* Beginning Business Letter Writing *into
the back of a pickup. Warren pulled out and I put the wig
on my head and a straw hat and ducked as we passed the
bus. When we got on the highway I changed the white
prison shirt and pants for jeans and an old shirt and my
yellow boots and told Warren I was sure enough born
again.*

Warren headed northeast toward Texarkana telling me for sixty miles how I'm crazy and I said, yeah, man, but knowing I had to do it. After a while Warren shut up. I looked out the window at those loblolly pines and red dirt hills wanting to get out and run free for about forty miles just to see how it felt. We listened to music and had a smoke and drank the six-pack. Before long we were seeing bumperstickers saying "Texarkana Is Twice As Nice." I told Warren nobody but the Indians was ever so glad to get out of Texas. I bought a one-way ticket to D.C. and took the chord organ and the Venezuelan flight bag and told Warren he'd be hearing from me.

The bus only leaves twice a day for D.C. so I waited across the street in a bar and grill to avoid cops grousing around the bus station trying to get their quota. When the bus finally pulled out of Texarkana, even Arkansas was smiling. Then all the way people kept wanting to talk just till they got to Little Rock, to Memphis, to Roanoke, to Richmond.

Outside Roanoke I began to feel like my life was circling around since I knew we'd pass not a mile from Merle's trailer house. I'd forgotten how tall the trees are in Virginia, tall and overgrown like me, oaks and elm and pine and creeper climbing over hills and houses and even old cars, so you feel like you might wake up some morning wound up and growing into the ground. Merle works as a practical nurse and Robert, when he works, as a utility man in a factory. The last summer I was with them I was supposed to be finishing school: "You're a smart boy,"

Merle was always saying to me, "learned to read in the first grade." *That was before she started gliding us around the country like the Ice Capades taking off with one man or another, parking me in movie theatres when I was in the way. Never learned multiplication. Some nights when we were in Virginia I'd sleep in an old hammock and look up at the trees, letting my mind blow free like the squirrels leaping from limb to limb never touching the ground. It was better outside. Inside it was canned alive with the sound of everybody's TV going at once. Merle would sometimes bring a chair out and sit with me till Robert would holler at her and she'd go back inside talking about daisies and reminding herself that even Robert was better than nobody.*

I got a job sacking groceries and met a guy who said he might get me a job playing organ at a funeral home. Then one night when I was sleeping in the hammock Robert butted me in the head with his knee. Merle was inside probably passed out. I told him that was some super shit way to wake up. I fought him back till he fell down. The next day Merle got up crying and told me to go. To go while Robert was gone to the shopping center for a bottle. It was getting winter anyway soon and it would be too crowded inside there with the three of us. So we got the chord organ out from where it was hidden behind the skirt of the trailer, Merle crying all the time. Merle could never stop herself crying. She cried watching the Billy Graham Crusade and the Miss Teenage America Contest. "I know I ain't done much for ya, Tennessee. I tried though. You remember that," *she said hugging me. She only came up to my collar bone and her breath was sour from the liquor and bad teeth that hurt a lot till she was having them pulled out, one by one like fence posts falling, leaving more and more gap. I knew she didn't want me coming back. She said she'd been thinking about sending me off for a while. Had worried about it. Asked the Lord to tell her when. But in the end Robert told her with his meanness.* "I'm not gettin' any younger, Tennessee," *she said.* "I gotta think of my old age. Wouldn't call me beautiful no longer." *Someone had once, in a bar back in West Virginia.*

She handed me seventeen dollars and told me to make good with my music. "You're a right nice looking boy, Tennessee. Don't let your teeth go bad. Maybe you'll be one of them boys that gets rich and comes back and builds his mama a new house." *She gave me a pat and I picked up the chord organ and the Venezuelan airline bag she'd found in a laundromat and walked off past the jacked up metal houses with the hose feeding into the sides like patients, past the office and the laundromat and the line of new mobile homes with curtains and For Sale signs in the windows. It wasn't fifteen minutes till I got a ride in an air-conditioned Buick with an old cassette tape playing "I Left My Heart in San Francisco." The man asked where I was headed. I started to say West Virginia but Merle always said don't ever go back to where you come from no matter what the song says, 'cause it's so different when you get back it's like it ain't there anymore. So I told him I was going to California.*

The man was heavy-set, wore an organization ring with

a diamond in it. "You got a ways to go, young man," *he said. I knew what he meant. Then he began telling me about his grandson straight and shiny as a pistol now with his braces off and starting into the Virginia Military Institute that fall.*

He let me off outside Richmond on 64 and I started walking up the highway thinking about California and just whomp! like a cymbal I knew something good was gonna happen there. I'd sell songs strong enough to end the world. Even get a mailing address.

That was nearly two years ago.

When the bus pulled into Richmond it was just getting light and I thought about Merle not so many miles away probably just getting off the nurses' night shift, standing on the corner sipping Styrofoam-flavored coffee as she waited for Robert to pick her up. For a minute I thought it might be nice to see her, just look in on her without her knowing. But I knew there's a time and a place and that wasn't it.

The bus was four hours late making D.C. about nine in the morning, the sun like a big red ball bowling toward the Capitol dome and everybody hurrying, even the pigeons. After Ferguson it was like arriving in the middle of everyone else's life. For a minute I could hardly remember who I was or used to be or what the sweet fuck I was gonna do next. Then standing outside the Greyhound station I thought about how I could hear some real live music or take in a movie or climb to the top of the Washington Monument and spit a mile or even rent a room and be alone for the first time in months. Then I saw a Kodak blue car with big

*chrome teeth and I remembered California and Claudie
and the kid and I felt something like a zipper pulling in my
stomach. So I said, move, man, knowing you don't stand
around bus stations like you can't decide what you're doing
unless you want somebody to make up your mind for you.*

*Down the block I found a phone booth in a McDonald's
and looked up* P . . . George Perry. *Then I found a man in
a white suit and said,* "Point me out Connecticut Avenue,
my man." *The man in the white suit says,* "You pass the
man's White House and Lafayette Park . . ."

"Now you ever hear of a rock band called Lost in
Space?" *I asked him.*

"How do you feel?" Elizabeth is asking. She is sitting on the side of the bed smoking one of her brown cigarettes, the nylon straps of her beige gown crossing the light horizontal strip of untanned skin across the center of her back. The door to the living room is closed. It is Saturday.

"You could have been killed, George, if you'd fallen into the excavation. It was really lucky he was behind you."

He? Who? George can't remember. There is a vague ache everywhere and a great dryness. When he wrinkles his forehead it hurts. When he tries to swallow his throat feels as though he'd smoked a thousand cigarettes the night before. "Who?" he manages to get out.

"Tennessee Blue. The guy that brought you in. He said it was lucky he was there."

Luck or something else, George thinks, remembering. Remembering the tall, slender figure behind him.

"He was nice to bring you home. After you went to bed he played some of his music. He's interesting."

You're interesting, George thinks. Interesting and magical and the kid is weird and unwanted and maybe dangerous.

"He was following me. I think he mugged me."

"Why would he then bring you home?" Her face is alarmed behind the cigarette. "And besides he doesn't seem the type."

"Maybe he wanted to meet you," George says and Elizabeth laughs and stubs her cigarette, leans over him, examining wounds he is just discovering, letting one small breast nearly kiss his sore cheek.

She touches his face. "I'm sorry," she says. "You should have let me call the police."

"Wouldn't have done any good."

It was a simple mugging, his first. Like being a virgin not having been mugged nowadays. He has heard many a man speak of the experience with the same pride men once told war stories.

"A lot of effort for twelve dollars," he says to Elizabeth, shifting in bed to touch her knee under the cool nylon of her gown.

"And a wristwatch," she adds.

Oh yes, a wristwatch, of course. A gift from Maureen and Claudie one bad Christmas.

"You don't think he really . . ."

"I don't know," he says and Elizabeth kisses him lightly and turns away, walks to the closet, lifting her gown over her head as she moves. She is too thin, as thin as Maureen always wanted to be. He admires her careless nakedness until she disappears and then he closes his eyes, the sound of her voice soothing him, her concern, her attention, her touch could heal him of anything, even leprosy. He wishes for the strength to look at himself. He imagines Dorian Gray—brown peeling edges and boils.

Elizabeth returns to the doorway and confesses uneasily, "George. Tennessee slept on the couch. He's going to do a mural in the hall. For a few meals. He needs them. I had no idea you might not trust him."

George groans, raises a hand to his forehead.

She turns away, begins brushing her teeth in the nice deliberate way she does things. Maureen always brushed her teeth as though she were mad at them. In a moment he hears her tap the brush against the sink and then he hears the shower and lies there enjoying the intimacy of the sounds. But finally the curiosity is too much. He brings himself up and realizes he doesn't feel too bad. The long mirror on the closet door shows him much the same— cautious, square face, beginning-to-gray brown hair, the slightest cleft in the chin, which he's always taken some pride in. The only evidence of the previous night is a bruise on one cheek and a slight scratch on the jaw. The face is no more puffy than it would be from an ordinary hangover. He feels disappointed. Suddenly he remembers his last sight of Claudie's face and turns away. He wraps himself in his bathrobe and ties it over the solid paunch of his stomach, then opens the door to the living room. Tennessee's long sleeping body is folded on the couch under a blanket, the blue organ open beside the coffee table. A straw cowboy hat hangs from a lamp. A mound of bushy brown hair lies on the floor, detached. *Jesus!* George thinks. What have we here? He considers possibilities—an ex-con, a Marine recruit? Ringworm?

Making no attempt at quiet George passes through to the kitchen and runs water for coffee watching Tennessee wake and rise, moving immediately like a child or a dog. When George puts the kettle on the fire and turns around Tennessee is standing in the doorway of the kitchen, his bushy-haired wig not many inches from the top of the frame.

"Thanks for helping me last night," George says, his tone less grateful than suspicious.

"Lucky I was there."

Elizabeth enters, neat and scrubbed as a shell, her brown hair wet and combed straight. She can read his distrust of Tennessee like a cue card held in the window. She passes George again and again as she brews her espresso and blends the awful health food soup she makes herself each morning, without touching him, the wounded. Tennessee says he'd like to try the soup sometime and she begins mixing one for him like a chemist while they discuss music and San Francisco and what Tennessee calls "meetin' folks." George sits silently drinking his instant coffee and instant breakfast, half turned away from the table, holding last week's news magazine, trying to read. And Elizabeth brings paper, his paper with "from the Department of Housing and Urban Development" on the top, for Tennessee to begin sketching a mural for the hall while he watches out of one eye that feels swollen thinking he doesn't want to live with a mural by Tennessee Blue even if it is Elizabeth's apartment. He sees Tennessee's pale face rising like dough to Elizabeth's friendliness, his eyes bright on her, too bright, surely injected with artificial coloring like supermarket fruit.

"Do you wear contact lenses?" George asks him.

They both stare at him as though he's had a seizure and Tennessee declares his eyes are 20/20. George wanders into the living room carrying coffee and the *Newsweek* of last week and tries to read an article on another nation's declining economy while Tennessee begins his autobiography there in the kitchen, the two of them sipping the health food glop while Tennessee tells about his life in the small towns of West Virginia.

In the afternoon Tennessee watches "Star Trek" reruns while George, typewriter on the kitchen table, writes to an employment service.

Make a Career-Switch NOW!!!!
Go
OVERSEAS
or to a choice area such as
Florida, Texas, Arizona, Hawaii

"Would you go with me, Elizabeth?" George calls.

"How about Hawaii? We could live on the beach, climb volcanos, ride the waves."

It is warm. The windows are open so that the sounds of the city invade the room between blasts from the Starship *Enterprise*. Elizabeth smiles and turns back to the book she is reading, glancing up occasionally at "Star Trek."

MEN/WOMEN
Changing Careers or Job Seeking?

Midstream Employment specializes in mid-career changes for men and women seeking greater rewards by transferring their skills into other fields of the media.

call/write

They are mad for diagonals, this company. Is it a secret code of homosexuality? An occult sect? A sign of weakness? Simply a lack of commitment?

Elizabeth turns the page without looking up. She is a mystery reader. A reader of novels and poetry.

"Don't read poetry," he sometimes says to her.

"Why not, George?"

"It makes me nervous," he says.

Dear Midstream People:

I am attracted to your ad because I am indeed mid. Mid of career, life, heart and mind. So I come to you offering what remains. Attached please find my résumé which will give you the bare, essential facts—my life in nude, as it were—which has little to do with me or my life as I've lived it. Facts are so apart from life, reveal so little.

You will note that I was born in Wisconsin. We moved six months later, so forget Wisconsin. You will see that I have a college degree. Forget that, too. I don't think I learned a thing except the natural arts of drinking and screwing, journalism being a subject less substantial than palm reading. There is, too, a record of past employment in various locales—Milwaukee, Des Moines, Nashville and finally Washington. Not a bad city over the years, Washington. I knew it when they rolled up the streets. It's not like that now, never was really if you knew where to go. At Teddy's Pastel Room they never rolled up anything except a few patrons now and then. But I didn't always know that, having been a proper suburbanite with rules and habits and regular and balanced meals. And then, dear Midstream, then came the time, the spot recorded on my palm where the line breaks, the watershed of my professional life, as they say. Into the office one muggy morning, cheery as such a routine-bearing slave could be, when the sky falls, the earth stops, the door to every bar in town must have shuddered. The good daily rag was dead, passing in secret, in the hush of night, and the boys were out, hundreds of us jamming the bars, crying up the alleys, swerving along every commuter road into Maryland and Virginia.

What to do? It's not just that every third person on the street is a pundit but now the other two are out-of-work reporters. So one starts swinging the hat wide and throwing the lariat far. Reaching: Assistant Director, News Services Division, Department of Housing and Urban Development, that great open-wide-the-arms building on Seventh Southwest where I fed at the trough for six years learning the system, learning that government is against us individuals, but we all know that. We all ride the tiger.

It was not so bad after a while, after becoming accustomed to the bureaucratic ambiance, much the same reign-of-terror atmosphere as a home for retarded boys—foolishness and waste and stymied minds caught in the hum of the giant machine. And so after personal upheaval, I left. Walking into the offices of the Committee on Banking and Currency of the House and delivering into their in-box laps material which should have made the nation blush. It did not. But that is another story and on with the facts.

Political affiliation? Skeptic. Too old for the fun of the raucous Sixties. I fell in a crack there, since I don't fit the generation before either. We're a lost group, we mid-forty people. Should be studied, polled, queried and pickled for posterity.

And so you see, Midstream, with mid-life comes not bitterness but realization, calm realization, having breathed and composed the rancid farts of government too long to be impetuous or proud. And so here it is, flat out, black and white. I leave you to your own conclusions.

And so with hope for the future I remain, job seekingly,

George Perry

George pulls the paper from the typewriter. The Starship *Enterprise* blasts off safely and a commercial appears. Tennessee rises, stretches, so that his fingers touch the ceiling. The wig surprisingly hangs in place. He picks up the blue chord organ.

"Sure appreciate everything," he says to Elizabeth and heads for the door.

George punches the spacer on the typewriter and calls after him, "Care to tell me why you were following me last night?"

Tennessee pauses, turns, faces George thoughtfully. "Well, I had a feeling since I first saw you. I said this man is ready for the great gates and the open sound but he may not be prepared." He nods as if that's a perfectly clear explanation. And then he's gone.

At 11:25 A.M. Sunday George is before the TV. It is
five minutes early but he switches on anyway, thinking he
might catch her as he once did, the camera on her
unprepared, then the amazing switch of her face, a lamp
turning on, when she saw the red light. Sometimes he
believes he catches the last thread of smoke from her
cigarette, and he imagines her snuffing it out at the last
moment. And suddenly there she is, smiling, not too
much, just right. She has it all down now and she looks
good, not soft or young but good. The face that is all mouth
and sharp nose and large eyes, those wide jaws, that she
thought ugly once, are *de rigueur* for women in TV. And
there's the voice, the voice he heard daily for more than
sixteen years, only it's changed. It is more controlled,
lower, professionally confident. He listens for the slight

uneasy rise he used to know. It is never there. Each Sunday he waits for that sign of weakness and hates himself for waiting.

Elizabeth enters in panties and an unbuttoned blouse, brushing her hair and rubbing her scalp with something that smells like lemon.

"Hello there, Maureen," she says to the woman she's only met via video. "Nice blouse. I think she's got on a skirt today, George."

She stands beside him and he turns his head and smells their recent love-making on her. It is what they do on Sunday mornings in the light, which Maureen never liked. Elizabeth, loving him with coffee mugs and newspapers around the bed. Elizabeth lying nude, eating, croissant crumbs falling onto her breasts.

"I think I'll leave you two alone," she says. It is as close as she ever comes to saying anything sarcastic about Maureen. He knows the two of them have sympathy for one another as though their both having experienced him, like having fought in some common war, even on opposite sides, gives them respect for one another.

When he hears the shower he speaks. "Maureen," he says aloud. Saying her name makes the room feel strange and unfamiliar, though he's noticed no room seems truly familiar anymore. He tries to integrate the TV image with those in his mind—Maureen beside him in the car, her hand on his leg, Maureen across the table drinking coffee from a blue cup, looking at him with accusing eyes; Maureen pregnant standing sideways in her slip smiling before the mirror, Maureen and the baby, like kangaroos, he'd thought, one entity; Maureen and Claudie reading nursery rhymes, *"I do not like thee Doctor Fell, the reason why I cannot tell."* And Maureen crying, her face turning to him with hatred.

She is interviewing a dancer. The woman's face is harsh and thin next to Maureen's. She speaks hesitantly until Maureen draws her out. *"The dance is finding new space . . . spaces that exist . . ."* Like me, George thinks, looking for space not to invade but to fit into, comfortably, without warfare or grief.

"And what do you think of the new body dance . . . ?" Maureen asks.

Once you couldn't have done this, Maureen. How did you learn, love? Did I really harness you all those years, suck the blood out, as you so delicately put it? You were never so diplomatic when interviewing me.

"Now when the relationship of dance to music is usually contrapuntal, why does your new dance flow, why is the movement nearly harmonious?"

Harmonious, surely an obscure word. But he can recall the idea, even the experience—a phonograph record playing over and over, a half bed in a small apartment in Winnetka, Illinois, harmonious movement in the classic manner. You were always very classic, Maureen.

"But the role of women choreographers . . . ," the dancer is saying and George wants to cover his ears, to protest at hearing week after week from each woman on

"Women in the Arts" the same sentiments. But he sits, a prisoner, until she announces next week's guest and says goodbye, smiling to all those anonymous thousands when he didn't get a smile like that for years. But her smile and she herself are nicer now and he regrets that she is nearly beautiful without him even if he doesn't want her anymore. And he doesn't, he admits, most of the time anyway. It's just that he is a classic person, too, and habits linger.

He rises and mixes himself a bourbon on ice and pours some coffee so he won't drink the bourbon too fast. He sits back and watches the blank screen of the TV which is the way he visualizes his mind most of the time and thinks about Maureen and Claudie. Claudie, of sixteen brief summers, small and neat, her face sweet as a flower, her body thin and gentle as a blade of grass. She demanded little. They demanded: affection, reason, consciousness of time, energy and direction, all of which seem not too important to him now. Their conversation dwindled to common phrases as though read from a Berlitz handbook. *Pass the salt, please.* Although as a child she had talked early. *When the wind blows the baby will fly,* she'd sung at two, knowing already. Kind, generous, Claudie.

"And who is the girl in the bedroom wearing the big hat who won't speak or come out?"

"That's Jenny. I ran into her. Some man started to attack her so she jumped out of the car."

"Attack her!"

"Yes."

"Why didn't she go to the police?" Lights, sirens, detectives, Mr. District Attorney, champion of the people!

"*Dad, Jenny didn't wanna do that. It really happened to her once before and she went to the police and they didn't do anything.*"

"*Oh, Claudie,*" he said, the words sagging with skepticism. He didn't believe her, but she never lied. There was just so much between the truth and the lie and they never took the time to explore the inbetween.

Jenny. A year or so older than Claudie from a big family in rural Maryland. Her father was dead. She'd come to D.C. to work her way through community college. Could she stay a week or so, till she found a place, Claudie asked? So Jenny settled in. A street and night creature. She carried all her belongings in a large purse except she claimed she had an old fox coat in department store storage. Her face was serene and sweet under the wide hat and her breasts billowed disconcertingly under her blouse. Looking at her made George uneasy. *Oh, wow!* he found himself thinking, which was Jenny's own constant phrase.

Maureen was patient and generous. Jenny was a disadvantaged girl who'd suffered. Them against us, that kind of thing. It made George feel even more uncomfortable.

"*What happened with Jenny last night?*" he asked, having heard their voices in the night.

"*Somebody tried to rape her,*" Claudie said. "*Some man picked her up when she was hitchhiking to work and . . .*"

"*Hitchhiking!*" he roared. "*Claudie, my God!*"

"*But it's two hours by bus to Georgetown,*" Claudie cried.

"*Hitchhiking! Whatta you expect, hitchhiking!*"

She was calm. *"I don't expect that. I don't expect one person to attack another person or steal from another person or murder another person. I don't expect it. Are you asking me to expect it?"*

"You're damn right you should expect it! Hitchhiking around here . . . in a city! As if you don't run into enough trouble nowadays sitting in your living room."

Claudie turned away.

Quietly one evening Maureen confided to him. *"She told Claudie that at her last job where she was a live-in babysitter, her employer tried to rape her."*

George felt a rage in him like a bonfire leaping forth singeing the trees above. *"Get her out,"* he said. *"Just get her out."*

Claudie confronted him later. *"She can't help it if people are always trying to attack her."*

"Do you believe it?"

"Yes." She stood very small and straight, her bare feet braced on the brick patio where they stood. She seemed very strong. She always seemed strong, her actions deliberate. She was not one of those hopeless waifs. It was something he couldn't reconcile later. He knew it was partly her strength that led her away.

"Well, she's screwed up, that's for sure," he said. It was not a thoughtful choice of words. It put him in the tribe of barbarians, those in buffalo hides sweeping through the struggling world, defiling innocent minds, betraying the helpless and homeless.

"Just get her out," he shouted and would say no more.

Jenny left Maureen a thank-you note decorated with

delicately drawn flowers signed *"love and peace, jenny."* After that Claudie stayed away most of the time. Then one witheringly hot Saturday afternoon as he was watching the Mets in L.A. she came in to announce she had decided not to finish school. She was going to California to work in films.

"That's an awful idea!" Maureen called from the hallway. Later she said, of course, she'd thought Claudie was talking about acting, becoming a movie star. Maureen entered the room carrying the mail and seeing how serious Claudie looked standing in her cutoff jeans and a KISS T-shirt, Maureen laughed. George had always thought that laugh cost Maureen. It was the reason Claudie had always phoned him and asked him for help. He and Claudie had always been closer. There was some kind of jealousy between Maureen and Claudie. Always had been. And lately Maureen had gotten in the habit of restaging her quarrels with Claudie before him, bringing them up in summary form knowing he too would join in the criticism and therefore assembling forces against her. It wasn't fair and George had realized that but hadn't felt strongly enough or found the right moment to stop it. Now he saw something cold and unforgiving in Claudie's face as she watched her mother laugh and turn away. She addressed the rest of her remarks to him.

She decided that she might like a career in film editing but the only way to learn film work was to apprentice to a union member. That's what she wanted to do.

"Surely there's a way to work in film and get an

education, too," he said casually, his eyes back on the ball game.

"That's an education," she said. *"Everybody doesn't have to go to college to get educated. It's just a middle-class status symbol,"* she said, leaving herself open to Maureen's, *"Oh, Claudie!"* shaking her head as if she'd never heard anything so foolish.

Neither of them was looking at Claudie when she left the room. His eyes were on the ball game. Maureen had opened her new *Gourmet* magazine. And Claudie's retreating feet made no sound on the carpeting.

A week later she was gone. Her bed made neatly, the windows closed in case of rain. Such a neat disappearance had been planned like a letter of complaint finally written. Everyone dreams of running away, George thought, now the young do. And she was gone for good, the room stripped clean, the discarded personal effects stuffed into a plastic garbage bag behind the garage and labeled GOODWILL. Even ice skates. The room left empty as the moon as though her existence there had never been except for the note. *"Don't worry. I'll phone soon. Claudie."*

"Mother!" He kept hearing Claudie's voice calling through the empty house after she was gone.

George and Maureen followed what they discovered was the usual middle-class ritual. They contacted "the authorities." They visited various run-away houses in the area and asked greasy-haired kids with foggy eyes if they'd seen Claudie—nearly seventeen, five foot four, blonde hair, green eyes, slender build. They talked to directors of such houses who very often looked like copies of the kids, who spoke in the single-syllable jargon of the young or the multi-syllabic jargon of their professional training, both unintelligible and usually infuriating to George. They attended meetings with other parents of runaways. George flew to Los Angeles and hired a skinny private detective who wore white gloves to hide the eczema on his hands who specialized in tracking runaways. They learned that of the thousands of runaways each year some return home, usually within four days, some are lost to drugs, some lured or forced into prostitution, a small percentage murdered. The general picture eventually broke down into individual stories as they grew to know other parents: The father whose daughter finally returned with her teeth knocked out, after, he said, only a few brief years earlier he'd spent thousands of dollars on orthodontists and braces. The father afterwards embarrassed at his complaint and then shrugging as if to say, what in hell *do* you say.

He and Maureen read books and discussed their failure and meanwhile the guilt grew on them each time they passed her empty room, the evidence, exhibit A of the irrelevance of order and physical security. Exhibit B of their inability to understand, to share themselves, even to have known the wealth of her presence.

After a month she phoned to say she was all right. She was sorry they'd worried. She would have left home one day, just think of her as having left earlier, she suggested. She was in California. She had a job working in a film lab.

She could learn a lot there. She would phone again soon. It was not so long ago. Not even two years ago.

And so he and Maureen dwelled unhappily with their guilt and loss and loneliness and began to notice one another and the separation that had been going on over the years. Maureen never meeting his eyes, inhibited with him. He was a vague object, a person across the table, an arm extended offering coffee, a warm body in bed. And now there was all the more reason not to meet his eyes because she didn't want to see his claim, sympathize with his grief. She might have responded to it and she didn't want to. It was all those years of resistance to her own dependence, building up until she couldn't get through any longer without chiseling pain. Much easier it would be to start over with someone new, someone who did not share the role of co-conspirator in guilt and grief, who might even offer a new liberty. And once she realized that Claudie wasn't coming back, the door was open and Maureen wandered out, frightened at first, half-heartedly like a kitten but soon with confidence, and she stayed on and on and on. Whatever he said didn't matter anymore. And right outside was Grey. *"I've always liked poetry,"* she said when George urged upon her a new "interest" so she signed on the dotted line. And Grey, young and writing poetry—"timeless as air," he wrote her—was willing to share more than insights into Contemporary Poetry.

George, helpless, watched the passion grow like a pregnancy. And to fall into Grey's bed was like finding the fountain of youth. She revived. Her skin grew young. Soft smiles long lost returned. George watched with awe and pain. Claudie is gone so why not swim in that fountain of youth every night! turn your back on all those possessions you've been collecting to make up for the years. So she sold her antiques, put on jeans and tied a scarf around her head like a kid and left, like Claudie.

And George, proclaiming the world gone mad, felt deep inside that she was right to go.

The phone rings. Elizabeth answers. George rises to get another drink and this time doesn't bother with coffee. He thinks of the last time Claudie phoned. A Sunday. Not even a year ago. It was always Sunday when Claudie would phone, collect, from God knows where. The last time it was late at night and there was the surprise of a male operator with a southwestern drawl.

Claudie: *"Hello, Dad."*

Then silence. She waited for him to talk. She always did that. *You phoned,* he wanted to yell, *you converse, tell me something! For God's sake where are you? What are you doing?* Her silence usually forced him into saying things he didn't want to say.

"And what can I do for you today?" he said that last night, all wrong, when he was thinking, *Claudie, my dear, my flower, were you here tonight I'd take you atop the Washington Hotel onto the terrace overlooking the putrid Potomac and amidst all that is unholy we would see beauty and I would bare my soul and speak of love, for you, for*

your mother, for Elizabeth, all the love I've known, not a lot but enough for a life, which is short, is it not?

"*Dad,*" she repeated. There was something wrong, he knew then. There was ice in her voice, fear, her breathing and speech were distorted.

"*I don't have anyone to talk to!*"

He was glad to hear from her, he said. "*What's wrong?*" he asked but she didn't seem to hear him. She was quiet again and for a moment he let the quiet sit there between them along with the miles while his mind jumped to conclusions and all the dangers he'd thought of how many times before.

"*What's the worst thing that can happen?*"

"*What do you mean? What's wrong?*" He couldn't answer her question, he didn't know what to say and he had to be honest, he'd learned that. Nothing off the top of your head for the serious young.

"*There's nobody here,*" she said. "*I can't hear you. I'm scared.*" And she was crying, sobbing, saying, "*Oh no, God, oh no, oh no . . .*" over and over.

He tried to shout questions through her crying. "*Where are you? Let me help you. What's wrong. What do you mean?*" She didn't seem to hear.

When she spoke again she was incoherent, trying to explain something to justify herself when he had no idea what she was talking about.

"*Freedom was the most important thing. That's what he said. It would save him, he said.*" And then she began sobbing again, the "*Oh no, oh no, God, oh no . . .*"

"Where are you, Claudie? What city? Give me the phone number there. Look at the numbers on the phone, Claudie."

Then the phone dropped. He heard it clunk against the side of the booth, then heard the door slide open and the sound of traffic as though it were coming into the booth. He imagined the receiver dangling there. He heard a truck pass.

He tried to trace the call. He cursed an operator, was cut off. Tried again. Waited, prayed. Cursed. They couldn't trace it.

George lifts his glass off the front page of the Sunday *Times*. It has sweated a dark circle around the head of a South African revolutionary. He finishes his drink and tries to interest himself in the news but it doesn't work. He stands, remembering how high Tennessee reached when he stretched. And suddenly he's afraid that Tennessee will return any minute.

"Elizabeth," he calls. "How 'bout a movie?"

Sunday night in the Ben-low Bar.

"Maybe Tennessee has disappeared into outer space," George says to Elizabeth across the table.

She smiles. His Elizabeth, though she is no one's, simply her own and much less his than most people have been, most people he's claimed anyway. His claiming ran them off, they said. He hears that but doesn't understand it. Elizabeth, the good-hearted, beige all over, the young body that loves his, who even knows him, seemed to know him from the start but still wants him . . . for a while. Honest, Elizabeth.

"George," she says now and touches his hand, "he phoned today and wanted us to come here tonight. His friends are playing."

George moans quietly and Elizabeth sips her drink, looking around expecting to see Tennessee in the crowded bar the way she had found George that night seven months ago in this very bar, by mistake. It turned out they shared the same building. She fed pigeons on the windowsill and never threw out a seed she could plant. After a while she took him in, freeing him from the loneliness and inefficiency of the furnished efficiency.

It was not just that he had been lonely and she had been lonely. After two minutes he was fascinated. Why? She was too skinny, her angular arms always surprised him. She was not pretty, but composed, satisfying to look at. She delighted him. Her hair, her talk, the rings she wore on her fingers, each detail of her, so that he had been clever with her, had made her laugh. And she had taken him seriously as a person, not just a lonely man looking for someone, as most women did. He *wasn't* looking for someone. He was still trying to stopper the wounds from Maureen, or at least understand. He had been testing the water of aloneness, dipping his toes, feeling nearly peaceful in the somber efficiency after the seesawing turmoil just past him.

Then Elizabeth. Why do certain people fit or satis-

fyingly collide? Why this woman, this demographer who
knew the number of unemployed miners and women heads
of households and single toilet houses in the United
States? What planetary guidance drew the two of them
together?

And she liked him. Claimed he had a voice like Steve
Canyon's. Had wanted him. Had hugged him with her thin
arms and held his hand and kissed his fingers and pressed
her thin body against him.

"So talk to me," she says now, pushing her hair out of
her eyes, never pinning it back sensibly, running her
graceful fingers with the narrow silver rings through it
repeatedly. She speaks affectedly like the young. No one
talks straight anymore like he does. He's never learned the
new ways. He tries to think of something to say. Maybe
he's getting too old to deal with women, he thinks. They
are too complicated.

"Once upon a time," he begins, "in this very bar, an
event of the centuries . . ."

She smiles and looks away. *You are fantasizing again,
George,* she is probably thinking. He can read it in her
eyes. She does not go for fantasy. She goes for mind
expansion, popular psychology, mild drugs, tranquility
through meditation and Vitamin-B something. But not
fantasy. *"Fantasy is out, George,"* she would probably say.
*"Gone the way of the buffalo, a few around for showing
children, but basically too big and impractical."*

"Like me, for instance," he'd say, and immediately feel
heavier, shaggy, pawing the earth. He felt that way often,

stepping carefully through his days with Elizabeth, never being his old, free, destructive buffalo self. He kept her constantly in his considering mind. He had to. There was much she would not tolerate—sentimentality, false words, a million of his male attitudes of old. It was worse than not smoking. Never for the rest of his life could he sing "The Girl That I Marry" to the girl he wanted to marry. Indeed he could not imagine how he could propose to her. How do you propose to a girl like Elizabeth, he wondered, looking at her. Maybe as you are renewing drivers' licenses you say, why not? It was tough this consideration, this monument of love in his mind, so different from what it had been with Maureen when it was laissez-faire, think of yourself, capitalistic love.

She is watching him now thoughtfully and he is pleased. Delighted to see her across from him, delighted even knowing she is willing to befriend the weird of the world like Tennessee Blue. So that now he wants to lean across the table and say one of those things he's not sure she'd want to hear. So he just looks at her and thinks *Stay with me, Elizabeth,* knowing that so much of that decision is up to him, a responsibility he's not certain he can live up to.

A group of young musicians in black jumpsuits are setting up instruments in the corner.

"Strange, men rarely perform alone," Elizabeth says, "and women nearly always do. You ever notice?"

The "notice" rises at the first syllable. She has a British inflection at times from spending six months in Maida Vale. Studying at the London School of Economics.

There were six-months lots of places because she is self-sufficient and curious. Willing to live with herself alone. It is maybe why her husband walked out one bright Sunday morning taking the Sunday papers and leaving the door unlocked.

"Why did he leave?" he had asked her, thinking the explanation might give him some clue to his own survival.

"We were never friends," she said.

"You weren't supposed to be friends, you were married," he said, only partially joking.

There is a siren sound and then the metallic roar of a computer game arcade leads into the music. The musicians are hairy with additional dark drawn diagonal eyebrows.

"Jesus!" he mutters toward Elizabeth but she is watching the band and the sound of the music wipes out every other. They are into a hard rock number, weird and driving that finally ends with a shrill dying whistle. The tall guitarist with fluffy blonde hair introduces the group as Lost in Space. They stare coolly at the crowded bar, noisy now without the music, the diagonal eyebrows, the shiny black jumpsuits setting them apart as though the small platform they stand on has set them on some strange land.

"This is the group Tennessee wanted us to hear!" George mutters.

On the next song the guitarist, standing under a green light, sings a song about the red glow of Mars, about faraway fields of unknown life. The green light gives him a deathly pallor and his voice has a throbbing, sinister tremolo.

"Let's go," George says to Elizabeth, "before they bring out snakes." But she smiles at him and lights one of her long cigarettes and watches the band. The next song begins with a soft, easy tempo.

When the blues are winning and the doors open in
When the sky is falling and you need a friend
If the San Andreas faults and all the oceans halt
Whatever happens, girl, I'll be right here,
    remembering the good times

Oh, Claudie, there is nothing that I wouldn't do for
    you
I'd take a trip to Mars and bring you back a star
Claudie, when your dreams run down I'll wind them
    up again,
Whatever happens, girl, I'll be around

The song is gentle. Not even ruined by the weird trembling voice of the guitarist. Of course, George thinks, of course. He takes a drink and listens.

When the ozone layer breaks, when every tree's a fake
Whatever happens, girl, I'll be around, remembering
    the good times

Claudie, there is nothing that I wouldn't do for you

He rises when he sees the tall figure in the cowboy hat at the back of the room and works his way through the tables to Tennessee standing alone. When George tries to speak to him above the pounding sound he shakes his bushy-wigged head. George motions toward the rear door and Tennessee moves down the corridor in front of him toward the red glow of the exit light, past the smell of frying potatoes, past a mirrored glimpse of his face still bruised and sore.

Outside Tennessee leans against a light colored sports car and lifts his hat and smooths his hair. George suddenly wonders if it is entirely wise to be in a dark alley with Tennessee.

"*Rolling Stone* says Lost in Space is the sound of the future—energy and ideas. Lots of spiritual presence. They liked to blew away the Rose Parade. Had hundreds of black balloons popping at the end of their numbers. Now they use tapes of missile launchings."

George can hear the band still singing Claudie's song.

"So you knew my daughter?"

Tennessee shifts his long legs and George thinks that he always seems to rehearse before he speaks. "Yeah, I sure did," he answers, looking George in the eye and then turning away and adding quietly, "I feel like I knew her all my life. Maybe before."

"It's a nice song. It sounds like her." It does, George thinks. It's a gentle song.

"She was a magic person."

When the last chances end, we'll start over again . . .

Tennessee sings quietly.

Whatever happens, girl, I'll be with you . . .

"I'd be interested in what you know about Claudie."
The invitation sounds like an investigation, like a cop or a
journalist. He tries to soften it. "I didn't know much about
her life the past couple of years . . . after she left home."
Nothing in fact, the great fill-in-the blank.

"I ran into her in San Francisco," Tennessee says.
"There was something special about her. I could tell right
away. I could see colors around her. There was a crowd of
people but I saw her. She was really there. You know?"

Two members of the band appear at the back door of
the club and signal to Tennessee. Tennessee waves and
George sees his eagerness to leave and wants to stop him,
hold him with force, anything.

"I see the men and ladies and old folks are calling,"
Tennessee says. "Catch you later."

"Sure."

George watches Tennessee saunter past a green dump-
ster and climb the steps to the Ben-low. He looks
incredibly strange and tall and out of place between the
two band members. One of them slaps his shoulder
affectionately and George feels as though he's standing in
the middle of a jigsaw puzzle. Suddenly his mouth is dry
and he wants a cigarette for the first time in months.

Above him the red lights of a plane rise over the
Potomac, nose up as though they were heading for the
moon. He swallows trying to relieve the dusty feeling in
his mouth and starts back inside for a drink.

Fireworks and all manner of magic. Oh, I could tell you in spades, George. About San Francisco. About walking up and down the pastel hills.

Oh, sit yourself down and tell me a secret
Maybe I could trust you then
Sit yourself down in your eight-piece suit

And I could tell you about Dan. The concert in the park on Lincoln Way. The Last Chances they called themselves. Red neck swing. Drawer-dropping, mind-bending music, Dan called it. The sound was new to me. Familiar but new. Like running into some uptown kinfolks, vaguely familiar but classy. Country with a touch of Barcelona. A little jazz underneath. Something of rock. Hard, a fist in the guts. I knew the sound in my head from then on and ever after would be different.

Dan the fiddler. Red beard and hair waving diamonds in the air. His fiddle making such music I could see the notes all colors, floating all the way to the Golden Gate and on past Alameda to the Pacific. On the vocals his voice spoke to the soul.

Once Merle dreamed Jesus arrived at Union Station smiling, wearing a brown suit and everyone in the world could see him at once. That was Dan. And Claudie was with him. She smiled and it was like two shots from a can of aerosol heaven. I couldn't move my eyes off her from then on.

"That's some fiddle," I said to her. "And I'm from West Virginia and that's where the angels play."

"He's great," she said.

I hung around while the Last Chances were putting their gear in the van. I told Dan I wrote songs like water runs. He wore silver bands on either wrist and a red bandanna around his neck. I asked where they were headed. He said Alameda and offered me a ride. I climbed into the van and never got out again.

There were five members of the group, sometimes six. We lived in a clean house in Alameda—clean 'cause Zook, the retarded drummer, liked to vacuum.

Claudie told me about her and Dan. How he'd first come to San Francisco in the Sixties. He'd known Janis and the 13th Floor Elevators, one of the early groups from Texas. He'd go back to Texas sometimes and roughneck in the oil fields. He had a tour in Vietnam. He had a wife one time, too, she said, but all he ever said about her was she wouldn't feed his dog. The truth is, Claudie said, there are years he can't remember. He nearly burned out his mind on acid. He says for ages he could close his eyes and watch movies on his eyelids. But now he's a peaceful man, she said, and things were working out real well. They'd just cut their first album, "Good Luck, Flower." Her picture was on the cover with them.

She told me she came to California to work in the movies. Not to act but to get into the other end of it, maybe editing. She said she'd grown up hanging around a Seven/Eleven in a suburb of Washington, D.C. Her mother collected antiques and her father worked for the government. They were nice enough people, she said, they just leaned on her a lot. She said they'd split up after she left, and maybe that was good.

Claudie was never mean, unlike Merle who had a mouth like a rattlesnake.

Claudie. Too bad you didn't know her, George. She was funny. Fun to be with. Pretty. Delicate like the inside of a watch.

And Dan was a party.

The group was under a peace bond not to play in the house but sometimes I could hear Dan fiddling for Claudie in their bedroom. It was enough to make a roach smile.

They were the first good friends I'd ever had. Merle and I had moved around so much I'd hardly learn a name before Merle would have us shuffling off somewhere else.

But Dan and Claudie were more than friends. I knew that. All my life Merle was always looking over one guy's shoulder into the next car. No one was ever satisfactory. For the first time I knew it didn't have to be like that. People could really like each other all the time.

Right away I started working as a shampooer for a unisex hair designer—Japanese style, kimonos and bare feet, playing tapes of Omsaka and his Oriental Rockers. Nights I started playing electric piano with Dan's group. And I was writing songs. Like "Meetin' the Good Luck Flower," or "The Girl with the Moon in Her Hands." And the sound began to come to me and stay, like finally getting to where you always wanted to be but didn't know it.

I could tell you so much it would change your life, George. Add a few daisies. And there ain't much time, since Warren says the cops are fanning out like the clap and any day there'll be a cop on the corner, leaping from a doorway and it'll be back to the shake downs and lock downs, watching for the prison patrol, waiting for the whistle to blow, lining up for plastic spoons and throwaway everything . . .

So, sit yourself down and tell me a secret
Maybe I can trust you then
Sit yourself down in your eight-piece suit
And I'll fill in the blanks for you

The next week Tennessee's strange drawings begin to cover the long hall. From the corner of George's eye the people, the creatures, the automobiles seem to move. Faced head on they hover. It is another world brought inside the apartment, greeting George each time he opens the door.

"I can't breathe in this hall anymore," George says. "It's like entering a nightmare."

"I like it," Elizabeth says. She is Tennessee's defender, his friend. Has given him a key so that he may come and go and keep dried fruit and papaya juice in the refrigerator. "It won't be for long," Elizabeth says, "till the mural is finished, a few days. He needs the money, George, and he needs friends."

"I saw a loose dog today, Elizabeth," George says.

"How about a few cats, a raccoon or two—they're clean? A few senior citizens?"

"I like the fiddler," Elizabeth says, pointing to the one recognizable figure in a corner playing a violin.

George looks again at the strange figure whose back is turned so that he seems to be playing away, into the past. He dreamed about that fiddler one night. Throughout the dream he'd tried to place the man but it wasn't until the next morning that he'd realized it was Tennessee's fiddler invading his dreams, as Tennessee is invading his life for some unknown purpose. His attempts at questioning Tennessee seem always to glide off into tales of West Virginia relatives struck by lightning or the Texas singer with three hundred and sixty-two self-administered tattoos or a new song about the problem of angels in outer space. His tales never settle on a single subject but wander about so that George sometimes forgets where they started.

"Well, Tennessee," George begins one night after they have shared steaks and salad and Sara Lee cheesecake, "I was thinking today of the fine old tradition of hospitality, of sharing meals and conversation and information." Tennessee and Elizabeth light cigarettes and George pulls out a mint and cracks it noisily between his teeth as he asks Tennessee to tell him about Claudie.

"Well, she was living in Alameda," Tennessee begins, "working at this film lab, learning all about it . . ." George eats two more mints while Tennessee talks about the lab. "And she met a man who'd been in pictures a long time and used to tell her about how so many things that happen in a film are actually accidents. Like this scary old movie where suddenly a white horse rears up, and they didn't expect it, but when they saw the rushes it scared the shit out of them so they left it in."

And Elizabeth says she remembers that movie which reminds her of the new thriller she'd like to see. And Tennessee allows as how he'd like to see that and before George can say what he is thinking which is, "By God, Tennessee, with such talents for evasion you should be Secretary of State!" they have checked the movie times and are out the door. George mutters and puts the dishes in the dishwasher and finishes the last piece of cheese-cake.

In the next few days George is convinced that Tennessee's few days could go on forever since he seems to have no sense of time, being perfectly content to sit on a park bench in Lafayette Park with a flock of pigeons or sit for hours writing in his notebook at an unattended sidewalk cafe so that George, finding him there one day, as he returns from a job interview, and then again hours later, wants to push Tennessee's pipelike body against the brick building and let the rain wash his face to some point of revelation. And then reaching nothing he might smash his narrow body in the gut, his fist right below the narrow rib cage.

Why? he asks, knowing himself a man not normally tuned to violence. Is he so jealous of the friendship with Elizabeth? Is it because Tennessee is at once gentle and secretive and suspect? He expects contradictions in those he knows, in adults, in his work. But he does not expect it in the young. Though knowing it was in Claudie, he avoids admitting it. Is it because Tennessee simply stirs the pool he's tried to settle for such a long time? Because the emotions Tennessee provokes make clear he himself has not changed, that were Claudie and Maureen to return he would once more rant and rave and fail?

Now late for an appointment, he passes Tennessee at the sidewalk cafe and hurries on.

"Had to kick two ladies and three men to keep this booth," Lawson says. He is a heavy man with a ruddy face whose upper body seems to be melting toward his middle. George settles across from him in the downtown bar filled with newsmen and bureaucrats. It is a simple bar, not formal enough for conducting business but easy enough for drinking with a friend after work.

"How's it going?" Lawson asks.

George shrugs. "Okay," he says. "Not good but not too bad."

Lawson is his friend from the Department. Since George left, they've not met regularly to discuss what is happening. Like most friendships made in working circumstances, he expects the relationship will gradually dissipate with lack of contact and common interests. Already he is seeing Lawson less often.

"How's Elizabeth?"

"Good. How's Marion?"

"Okay."

There is a moment of silence to allow Lawson to discuss his wife of twenty years if he wants. Lawson passes.

"Any news?"

"Not much," George says. "No fantastic offers."

"It's a hell of a note, isn't it?"

Lawson is part of the shadow department, one of the many leftovers of a previous administration or one who has been displeasing to the higher bureaucracy. They are shuffled aside, down the hall, into a corner, but never out. "Out" can virtually not be done. So their bodies line the halls and walls of every agency while their spirits contribute to the pall. It is what George escaped.

"How is Tucker getting on?" Tucker, a jaunty, short man with muttonchop sideburns. His was the position George might have had, had George not become a dissident.

"Still bustling about," Lawson answers.

"He'll slow down."

"The girls are calling him 'Jaws.'"

George chuckles. Sometimes there is simple justice in the horror of it all, the slow destruction of everyone. Nihilism, though unnamed, is rampant in the bureaucracy.

Lawson watches a blonde TV anchor woman pass, then turns back to George.

"I hear the Senator had fifty people apply for that P.R. spot. Did you consider it?"

"It takes young blood to be servile enough to suit a senator."

"Isn't that the truth," Lawson says. "I hear there are some shufflings at the *Post*."

"There are always shufflings at the *Post*," he says shaking his head, fearing he's had hardening of the bureaucratic arteries for too long. Real journalism would mean taking two steps back and competition with younger faces. And the money is bad. But the idea eats at the back of his mind.

"I did hear something you might be interested in." Lawson leans forward and George sees that he's been biding his time before passing on something hot.

"You remember Bud Schumaker? He's about to retire at Interior. He's got a pacemaker now and he can't take the summers anymore. I ran into him the other day. He asked about you. I told him you might be interested. He said to give him a call."

Lawson leans back to judge George's reaction. George lifts his vodka martini and wonders, what's interior? What does it mean? The bowels of the bureaucracy? Think of trees, George, he tells himself. Trees and parks. He's not sure of the relevance of trees and parks anymore but he speaks to please Lawson.

"That's a good thought."

"He's leaving in September," Lawson adds, "that is if he can survive another summer."

Survive. That is the question for us all. Under the influence of the vodka, September sounds years away and his own survival until then melancholy. "Well, I might not be around then," George says.

"Where?"

"Who knows?" He is thinking Hawaii, Arizona, Greece, Pago Pago.

He senses Lawson's disappointment but it is after all too much to ask for enthusiasm in the world and his share has surely been used up long ago. But to make amends he asks, "What's it like at Interior?"

"Not too bad," Lawson says. "Lots of environmental controversy, pleas from sufferers, pressure from despoilers, that kind of thing."

True, George thinks, there is much environmental suffering, his own environs that very moment being crowded with an unwanted guest and a weird mural he is powerless to control. Perhaps from the Interior Department he could at least control his own space.

The bar is getting louder and more relaxed. A girl laughs shrilly from a crowded table where a group is celebrating. George remembers the good feeling of stopping for a drink on Fridays, knowing the week's work is over. Now nothing is over except the days.

"Come home with me. Marion made spaghetti. Ask how I know?"

It is a joke, Marion's inevitable afternoon phone call.

Outside the traffic is backed up on 14th Street. On the corner a blind woman hits her old guitar while singing a tuneless gospel song. They hail a cab and head toward South Arlington amidst the Friday afternoon exodus.

Later George feels himself comfortably smashed coming back from Lawson's. Nothing out of control, just the
feeling of an easy, hazy distance between himself and the
rest of the world after having drunk too much and eaten too
much spaghetti and all that Marion Lawson serves with it
that makes herself and her husband and her two children
and even the dog and cat fat. If they had a snake, it would
be fat. The world, George decides looking out the cab's
smudged window, is divided by flesh. Not communism and
democracy, black and white, rich and poor. It's fat. He
sees himself looking through barbed wire, a concentration
camp victim. The Lawsons and everyone around him fat.
Elizabeth is on the other side near Maureen. Tennessee,
too. And Grey, of course, who even has a slim voice.

George sighs and decides it is unemployment that is
causing him to gain. Unemployment and frustration.
Proximity to leftover cheesecake. He glances at the thin
neck of the cab driver and swears he will cut down, then
diet to sleekness when he gets a job.

When he opens the apartment door a blue painted
rattlesnake greets him. Inside it is quiet except for the TV
but there is the smell of pot, a smell that seems
omnipresent to him these days. At the end of the hall he
finds Elizabeth and Tennessee side by side on the couch
watching TV, feet propped comfortably on the coffee
table, Tennessee's ridiculous yellow cowboy boots and
Elizabeth's bare, beloved feet. Seeing them together he
realizes that Tennessee is as close to Elizabeth's age as he
is. He hasn't thought of that before. They both look at him

uneasily and he feels his hostility flying through the air like the blue rattlesnake on the wall. He goes back to the closet and hangs his raincoat beside Tennessee's denim jacket. The animals on the wall seem to be stoned and flying through the smoke to attack him.

When he returns to the living room he realizes also that Elizabeth looks young and small like Claudie. Light hair, like Claudie. Small face, like Claudie. It is the first time he's realized they resemble each other in a way. The girl/woman he takes to bed is much like his own child. He finds the thought extraordinarily disturbing. But maybe it's not true, he tells himself. For a minute he's not sure he remembers how Claudie looked. Then he realizes he's standing in the doorway staring at them and muttering to himself.

"What is this?" he asks, with a tone of disapproval even he doesn't like, as he gestures toward the TV.

"King Kong," Elizabeth says. "The old one."

Elizabeth loves old movies. She analyzes their social content and places them within significant demographic patterns. They mostly bore him.

"How are you today, Tennessee? How were you yesterday and the day before?"

Tennessee looks at him sadly and then turns back to the TV where a flying animal is trying to take the girl from King Kong.

"Saw you following me yesterday. Saw you following me the day before. What are you, Tennessee, CIA?"

Elizabeth's look says a paragraph George would as

soon not read. It is not only disapproval but dread. *Please don't,* the look says. And he hesitates a moment. *Don't be a fool, George,* he tells himself, but he's already on his way. The alcohol has warmed his blood and is sending him hurtling along the path he's already begun.

The military is making plans to capture King Kong.

"How many bathrooms in *King Kong?*" he asks. "How many female-headed families?"

There is no response and he goes to the kitchen and mixes a drink. "Soda pop, Tennessee?" he calls. "Liquor, Elizabeth?" He mixes his own drink and returns. They have both lighted regular cigarettes and sit stiffly awaiting the firing squad.

"I gave up smoking, let's see now . . . how long ago?" His mind hazy, it takes him awhile to figure. "It was three months ago, no, three and a half."

Tennessee glances at him politely. Elizabeth stares at the TV, her chin tilted, defying attack. George has a vision of their own private doomsday clock, the minute hand jumping five minutes. There are only fifteen minutes left till destruction, maybe less. Actually they started at the half hour, never having a whole chance.

King Kong is in chains and growling.

George growls quietly and is surprised when he hears himself. It is easy to growl. He tries it again, louder and longer. They are both staring at him now. It gives him a sense of exhilaration, of power. He feels he has won over King Kong so he turns to Tennessee.

"I'm gonna get onto you like King Kong if you don't tell me about my daughter," he says.

Elizabeth's arms fold protectively across her breasts while her face closes like a door.

Tennessee faces him calmly. Through the alcohol fog he realizes that Tennessee has been afraid too many times, or perhaps not been afraid too many times, to be afraid of him—a white, middle-class, unemployed, middle-aged man, without even a single family dwelling to his name and largely drunk. He considers laughing at himself but can't, caught in his own absurdity knowing he will follow through till the miserable end.

On the TV *King Kong* is gone for a commercial.

"All right, damn you, tell me right now."

Tennessee's yellow boots draw back from the coffee table and he leans forward on his knees. "We were real good friends," Tennessee says.

The word "friends" is somehow different for him, George knows. It implies more importance than, say, his friend Lawson.

Tennessee moves his cigarette to his mouth and George sees again that look he's nearly come to expect, a studying, a worried scrutiny in Tennessee's eyes.

"We were the kind of friends that would take care of one another if . . ."

"When did you last see her?" George interrupts and Tennessee is silent a minute.

"I can't remember exactly," Tennessee says quietly. "About six months ago."

And what did she look like? Who was she with? What was she doing? He looks at Tennessee's accusing and troubled eyes and he feels suddenly sorry. He should have made friends with Tennessee. He should have been friends with him as he should have been friends with Claudie. Then he might find out those things.

George lifts his glass and drinks.

King Kong is on stage now. He roars and rattles his chains. The chains break. There is pandemonium.

Tennessee stands to leave. He seems incredibly tall.

"I'll tell you what happens," Elizabeth says dryly.

"I know," Tennessee says. "In movies monsters die. In life they follow you around in pickup trucks and kill you."

He moves toward the door and George calls after him. "She's dead. You know Claudie's dead?"

Tennessee doesn't turn around. "I know," he says.

At the sound of the door closing George feels suddenly deflated. Elizabeth is staring ahead woodenly at the TV. The monster is atop the Empire State Building, pathetically out of place, disproportionate with what is around him, while the world below hatefully clamors for vengeance.

Later he can't sleep for the faint whine of the TV and the accompanying whine of his own conscience. Elizabeth is watching *The Body Snatchers* on the late, late movie. He turns heavily, thinking he should get up and take some bubbly relief tablet knowing at the same time it is more than just stomach that is in discomfort. There are fears lurking far more real than any body snatcher. Elizabeth could that minute, with her split vision mind, be considering asking him to leave. Politely. Quietly without shouting she might say she no longer loves him. Love is not forever anymore, he knows. Egg on the face one morning and it's all over. He sits up and swings his legs off the bed. Elizabeth is curled up small on the couch. In the dim light she looks vulnerable and sad and standing in the door he feels willing to do anything to make up, to accept the flying animals in the hall, rattlesnakes, health food glop in the mornings, pot in the afternoon, anything to make them both happy again. He moves heavily past the TV and sits beside her. The movie is dark and old. He wants to ask her what is happening but doesn't feel he deserves to know. He simply sits beside her sipping Alka Seltzer.

"Why won't he tell me about Claudie?"

"I don't know." Her voice is soft and matter of fact. "Maybe because he knows you don't like him. You know you don't give people much of a chance. People who aren't like yourself."

"I gave you a chance."

"That was different."

"You think I'm jealous?"

"Yes."

"But I'm her father. And why the hell is he here?"

She pulls herself up and her voice changes so that she is not matter of fact at all. "Try being nice to him, George. For your own sake."

"But he's devious. He may even be dangerous." He realizes as soon as the words are out, that as soon as she's shown she really cares he's hardened his position and withdrawn. It is his pattern.

She sighs and turns back to the movie. "Have you considered that you might be narrow-minded and intolerant?" Her voice is again flat and matter of fact.

"That's what Claudie would have said."

She hides her face in her arms for a minute. "Oh, I'm sorry, George." She pulls herself close to him. "Let's watch the movie," she says.

He watches, not even knowing what is happening but thinking about her and how much he doesn't want to make her unhappy, wondering why she has to approve of him.

He waits for a commercial. "I'm the one who should be sorry," he says, not even sure any longer what he's sorry about.

She takes his hand and looks at him sadly. "It won't work like this, George. We're making one another unhappy too often."

Her words are like metal rods injected into his veins. "I know," he says.

"I'm glad you know, because if you know then whatever happens, you intend it to happen."

"*Oh, no!*" he says, but only to himself, unable to bring himself to once again disclaim responsibility for his actions.

"Can I get you a drink?" he offers.

She thanks him, grateful for very little.

He watches the whole bloody movie beside her, orderly and gentlemanly, willfully not kissing her neck or slipping his hand under her robe. But when they go to bed she moves into his arms and he sighs in celebration, feeling as though he's forcefully, with the sleek effort of a slim man, pushed their doomsday clock back maybe one minute.

"It's time to get a divorce," Maureen is saying lengthily. She's thought about it and thought about it and finally come to the decision.

"Congratulations," George says. "Someone said there is a time and place for everything."

"Yes, it was God, I think."

"Not God directly . . . ," George corrects.

"Let's be serious, George."

He agrees, not looking up from the martini, thinking, you are *always* serious Maureen.

It started badly. It was so surprising, her phoning, asking to see him. They had not spoken in months, only twice since Texas. It immediately gave him the feeling of preparing for the guillotine. But when they met her perfume was too strong. He was thrown off guard. Was it a conscious provocation? Was she trying to tell him something? In the least it was a clue to the real her beneath the smart dress, a reminder that he knew she wore talcum. That kind of knowledge is strength, he told himself, even to the unemployed.

She is reminding him of the subject. Sometimes they will not discuss one another's subject but now he gives in.

"You mean there's no good reason for a divorce, you just decided we might as well. What the hell! Let's divorce. I've never tried that before."

"Yes, it's simple, isn't it?"

She looks at him squarely, turning a head of revised hair. There is always something different and unfamiliar. He takes it as a personal affront since for years he had known every change if not before or the moment it was done, at least an hour afterwards. The hair is flattering and makes him want to look at her more than he wants to. He would like to tell her it is nice but doesn't dare. Theirs is still a power struggle.

"You're getting married," he says, thinking he can still read her mind.

She smiles because the accusation sounds old-fashioned. He intends to make *her* feel ridiculous but he has come out sounding like an old aunt.

"I don't know," she answers.

It is true, she doesn't lie and there's the new look again—square on, meeting his eyes unflinchingly, as though beneath those clear eyes, beyond the carefully drawn, nearly invisible makeup, the body and soul are empty of confusion and memory and love and all those threads that seem to be worming about inside him at all times. How can this happen, he wonders. According to joke and legend an ex-wife is always one to bully. Even the weakest, most unemployed man has that luxury.

He smiles at his own thoughts, which throws her off balance a minute, so he strikes. "How's Gaylord?"

It is a running insult. The name is *Grey*. New England waspish, he's charged, charging her with everything. *Grey*, how pretentious can you get, he'd shouted.

"We can't all be named GEORGE, can we?" she'd replied, winning hard on that one.

"He has a new book of poems coming out."

"Oh!" From the Weird Willington Press of Zapsville, no doubt. Nothing the man in the street ever heard of, but she and Grey are not concerned with the man in the street.

"How nice," he says.

She looks away, stabbing at the grapefruit in her diet salad and he has a chance to examine her, look for signs of collapse, but there are none. She finishes, arranges her fork across the salad plate with definition. Nothing halfway. She reaches for the ashtray at the same time he reaches for his drink and their hands nearly collide. But quickly, too quickly, she pulls back as though he's fire. Even the touch of his hand on her arm steering her to the table was unconstitutional. Her body made its rejoinder, straightening, pulling quickly as if it had been poked with a cattle prod. Was it that bad? he wondered, was touching him that unpleasant for her?

They had not touched in so long, except that once five months ago, surely the worst time between them. They were in Austin, their daughter dead, lying like an object on a slab, her face young and old at once. And Maureen beside him, both of them feeling like stones were raining down on them. Later at the hotel she began to cry, sobbing uncontrollably in a way that frightened him and he tried to comfort her, hold her, because of what had happened to them both. But she struck him hard in the face in that bright room with the open cosmetic case beside the bed, the mirror on its lid reflecting his stricken face when he turned away.

And now she is talking again, quietly, leaning over her plate, her elbow resting on the table, her hand with the cigarette swaying gently beside her face. She speaks of legal procedures and how she knows it is not a good time for him financially but it wouldn't be much. Already she has talked to a lawyer, a chic one who's dispatched some of the best men in town. And he hears the TV voice that goes out to anonymous thousands.

She is waiting for an answer, he realizes. Her question is there somehow in the air between them and her new, revised head has tilted questioningly. In the pause she moves the cigarette to her mouth and draws, looking at him as a stranger, one to be interviewed by a woman not under the influence of him at all.

He sits very still a moment, seeing his own largely self-imposed disadvantage clearly, and knowing it is his own adolescent summer riot, he takes his water glass, tall and stemmed and untouched, and tilts it until water rushes out the side of the glass and runs across the glossy wood table in a small rivulet past her diet salad and falls into the lap of her proper outfit.

There is something there then in her eyes, something personal, hatred, surprise but something. Then with hardly a sound, revealing the basically efficient creature that she is, she rises and pushes her chair back, opens her purse and tosses money onto the table. Then she walks away, quietly, ladylike, professional, her head high, centuries of resentment, carnage, and forgotten promises bracing her back like a steel beam. She would not have looked back, he knew, had there been a lion roaring at her heels.

George leaves the last personnel consultancy on his list and wonders what is next? Ice cream vendor? Domestic service? Welfare? He makes his way up the narrow walk in Georgetown crowded with teenagers and tourists and nomad vendors' tables stacked with candles and incense, jewelry and tacky Indian shirts, things Claudie might have bought. Everyone makes a living, don't they, he asks himself. He glances at his reflection in the darkened window of a restaurant and sees only an outline.

On the corner of M Street three young girls about Claudie's age when she left are playing baroque music on horns, the kind of thing Elizabeth loves. Elizabeth likes Bach. Bach sounds the way life should be, Elizabeth says. Mozart is too much to hope for.

He walks to what he considers the single decent bar in Georgetown, the only one not masquerading as an English pub or a French cafe and walks through to the men's room where a fly is buzzing inside. He holds the door open to let the fly sail out into the dark room.

At the bar he orders a double scotch and stares at the fragments of his face broken by bottles in the mirror across the bar. Why does he look at himself so much lately, he wonders. Maybe he is turning queer, he thinks. Then impetuously, before he can change his mind, he goes to the phone and dials.

"Bud Schumaker."

"Who's calling please?"

"King Kong."

"Just a minute, Mr. Kong."

The phone clicks to hold, the sound of nothing. He sees himself drifting in purgatory, passing lost souls shaped like doughnuts.

"I'm sorry but Mr. Schumaker is away from his desk at the moment."

"Tell him it's George Perry."

"Oh, . . . well . . . just a minute, please, I'll see if he's back."

Schumaker is laughing when he answers. "George, it's nice to hear from you. Lawson was mentioning you the other night."

So Lawson's been peddling me, George thinks.

"Glad you called. Say, I'm heading for a meeting right now, why don't we get together for lunch next week?" He hesitates and George hears him leafing through his calendar. "How about Tuesday?"

"Can't make it Tuesday," George lies.

"Let me see . . . ," Schumaker says. He rings his secretary, asks if a meeting is changed, and George considers hanging up, hating the bureaucrat in performance. Schumaker returns. "How about Thursday?"

Back at the bar George orders another drink and traces the events that brought him to that bar at 3:46 in the afternoon on a working day amidst retirees and financially independent alcoholics.

He had been at the Department long enough to appreciate the swagger of the true bureaucrat who knows it's they who hold the reins, not those up front who come and go. He had become somewhat accustomed to the excesses, the mindless repetition and reorganizations and unnecessary paper work that choked every office. He had seen Secretaries come and go and watched curiously as a new administration began a program to provide home-ownership for lower income families. Good idea, people said. Politically sound. It was the do-good era.

Shortly after the first year of the program the letters began arriving. "Dear Mr. Secretary . . ." They were polite at first. Homeowners all over the country were charging the government had inspected houses and approved loans for houses that later turned out to be unsound. The letters continued, increased. And one day an owner of such a house, a wiry black woman, appeared at the entrance to the agency wailing and shouting that the

Department was responsible for the deaths of her children in a fire that had engulfed her house while she was cleaning the floors of the Justice Department. She was subdued by a guard and held until the police could tote her wiry body across the river to that famous hospital for the disturbed and disturbing.

About that time the word "fraud" arose and George began looking into the situation. And later carrying a pile of letters and a memo outlining the activities of speculators in a burgeoning housing market, George walked down his yellow corridor to the orange corridor of the undersecretary who leaned on his plastic wood desk and told George in effect that it was the housing industry the Department was concerned with. The Department couldn't get involved in individual matters.

George left the color-coordinated office of the under-secretary but he did not leave the agency, though he did quit reading the letters from unhappy homeowners. He did not leave the agency even after his gradual and growing intransigence had left him with hardly any work and a new chief younger than himself with gold chains around his neck. Not even after he realized he was joining the ranks of the shadow bureaucracy—drinkers and troublemakers willing to stand in place through the years until retirement is secure.

Then finally, flying back from Austin after Claudie was dead and in the ground, feeling as though the weight of the plane was riding his own shoulders, he decided how he might repair something of himself. So he assembled

information and then one bright winter day when the gray
Potomac looked like the Aegean from a distance, he left
the agency, taking his accrued retirement, and went to the
Hill and dropped a thick file on the desk of the House
Banking and Currency Committee currently looking into
thousands of abandoned and condemned houses with
FHA-backed loans that the government was suddenly
falling heir to.

And now George orders another drink and realizes he
is getting expensively drunk when he could buy a bottle
and get drunk in a more economical fashion. The unemployed simply cannot afford to get drunk in bars.

He pays his tab and rises to leave. Four dusty and
leathery young men in motorcycle outfits gathered around
a table of beer and pizza are singing loudly with the
jukebox . . .

Just gettin' by on gettin' by's my stock in trade
Livin' it day to day, pickin' up the pieces wherever
        they fall
Just lettin' it roll, lettin' the high times carry the low
Just livin' my life easy come easy go

The next day Elizabeth is gone when George wakes.
There is light through the blinds like a fire outside. When
he walks to the window he sees it is a rare day, bright and
clear. On the macadam and gravel roof of the building
across the alley, a young girl is watering five young tomato

plants lined in deep green metal pots. She is a student, George thinks, because sometimes during a warm and sunny day she brings a chair to the roof and sits beside her tomato plants and reads with a pen in one hand. Then again maybe she works nights, perhaps at one of the massage parlors, as handy now as the corner drugstore. He thinks of her leaning over reclining flesh, her warm body casting the slightest fragrance of tomato about the small cubicle and sending some unwary customer into tears of nostalgia for his youth and lost innocence. Or tears of joy, since no one regrets the loss of innocence. Surely that is a myth if there ever was one.

The girl has finished watering now and departed and George vows he'll send her plant food from the Interior Department should he ever belong there, with a note expressing his admiration for her conscientious attitude toward her tomato plants. In fact, he decides, should he join the Interior Department he will strongly support city rooftop gardens. In concert with the Agriculture Department he will advocate the cultivation of acres of city roofs throughout the nation thereby improving individual economies and the general environment. The Perry City Farming Plan. He imagines the roofs within view of him lush, tropical and inviting. Elevator marquees detailing that building's particular crop and yield.

Leaving the bedroom he catches Tennessee on his way out wearing red suspenders over a T-shirt that has an armadillo on it. As George pointed out to Elizabeth the night before, Tennessee has been there over a week. The thought makes him mad in the pit of his stomach where it is easy to get mad early in the morning.

"I'm staying in this morning to work on my book," he announces staring out the window that is mostly opaque with Elizabeth's plants.

"Why, hey I didn't know you were writing a book?" Tennessee drawls excitedly, putting on his hat.

"A sex book," George says, *"The Indomitable Male."*

George lifts a spoon of instant coffee toward a mug and spills it onto a small puddle of water on the counter where it immediately grows into a brown blob like something deadly.

"'In*dom*itable.'" Tennessee tries out the word. "What would you mean by that?"

"You know, never a loser," George explains watching uncomfortably as Tennessee grasps the concept with some humor.

"Oh!" he says, and pondering a minute adds, "Don't think I ever knew anybody indomitable before. Even Hell's Angels move in packs. The Rhinestone Cowboy has body guards."

George lifts part of the brown blob into the mug with a knife and waits for the water to boil. "It's more a state of mind," George says, retreating.

"'Indomitable' is not even a good word for a song."

Tennessee begins to hum experimentally as he heads for the door. The water shrieks to a boil and George lifts the kettle.

"Well, have a good day!" Tennessee says in parting

and George wonders who the fuck started that line.

Later he finds it a day so pleasant as to melt furies and inspire forgiveness. He fails even to curse the Scientologists passing out literature on DuPont Circle. When he sees Tennessee coming out of a drugstore and heading up Connecticut Avenue, he isn't even annoyed as absurd as he looks in his red suspenders and his cowboy hat. He is no longer wearing his wig though his growing hair is curiously duplicating it. Still he looks otherworldly, George thinks, and without really deciding to do so, begins to follow. At the bridge over Rock Creek Park Tennessee spots him.

"What's happening?" Tennessee calls. "Thought you were waitin' on the muse."

"I didn't feel indomitable today," George says easily.

It has been years since George has been to a zoo. At the entrance Tennessee is caught up in a covey of school children wearing name tags. The children laugh and jump around him when Tennessee smiles and snaps his red suspenders, swaying his body as if there were music around him. Actually there is construction. A bulldozer nearby groans forward, pushing red earth. Workers are scattered about the area where some of the animals are missing, relocated during the renovation. A man in a blue blazer with a pink carnation in his lapel passes, whispering to a woman, reminding George of another zoo, of holding hands with Maureen, buying snow cones, Maureen's mouth scarlet and tasting of raspberry syrup.

Tennessee has paused outside the elephant house

where a pygmy hippo stands in a yard empty except for one pigeon. Nearby monkeys line a rope, their tails hanging in question marks.

"What'd you guys do to pull life?" Tennessee mutters to them. The monkeys chatter. "They oughta let 'em loose in the park. Might liven up the area," Tennessee says. "I can't understand why different creatures can't live together without fucking jails and bars?" He begins to walk away. "I don't guess you ever pulled time?" he asks George, glancing at him quickly.

"I was in ROTC," George says.

"Well, it's about like being one of these animals. And they treat you like an animal. Just as soon you were one. There's no good that can happen, let me tell you. You've got a choice of going crazy or drowning in your toilet."

They climb a hill with panda tracks painted on the walk and Tennessee picks a small blue flower.

"Sounds like firsthand experience," George says. "When was it?"

"Not long enough ago, I tell ya," Tennessee says.

He sticks the flower into a hole in his T-shirt so it hangs over the armadillo's ear. George feels some relief at the unsavory but first solid bit of information he's learned since Tennessee arrived.

"The last time Claudie phoned she said something awful had happened to her. She was crying."

Tennessee's eyes under the shade of his hat squint to narrow blue rods. "I didn't do anything to her. I just helped her do it to herself," he says.

In the brightness George can see him too clearly. His bony face that can switch from pleasure to despair with a word, looks old and hard and angry.

"You know sometimes something so heavy can happen to a person they just can't get over it," Tennessee says. "It just leans on 'em and doesn't stop."

"Most people feel like that at some time," George says, "but they do get over it eventually, don't they?"

"Some folks don't."

It is a rebuke and George is surprised and annoyed, knowing he's wrong. He thinks of Tennessee curling into himself with his secrets like one of the brown circles of fur sleeping in trees they are passing, a mysterious other species.

"When she got into trouble I tried to talk her into coming to you or her mother." He kicks a stone with a yellow boot and watches it scuttle down the path.

"Why didn't she?" George asks.

"She said she couldn't. Hell, she wouldn't even talk about it. I've spent a lot of time wondering why she wouldn't go home."

They stop on a small bridge and Tennessee leans on the side looking down to where an old peacock stops to look at them, tilting his head questioningly. He sways a moment then begins slowly to fan his ragged feathers, turning, performing shabbily before them in the sun.

"You might have fucking saved her," Tennessee says.

George doesn't reply. He turns and walks away hearing the loud, persistent bellow of a crane which drowns even the sound of the bulldozer.

I'd swear on a herd of angels. I did ask her to go to her folks. She said she'd left home and she wasn't going back. And besides it wasn't even there anymore.

"Wouldn't wanna say you're stubborn or anything."

"Then don't," *she said.*

I thought George coming along with me meant he was beginning to look outside himself. I thought the peacock might be a good sign. But he won't share. As much as he wants to know about Claudie, he's not offering anything back. He won't even admit mistakes. And one thing I know for sure, I've had my share of mistakes and more, and you have to admit them and live them. You walk the earth telling and remembering till you pay up. Or you can hold it inside like he's doing until you're all metal and dead.

I guess I feel like a fucking expert on mistakes. Things going from top to bottom. That's what happened to us.

We left San Francisco. Moved to L.A. Were living in a mission house in Santa Monica a few blocks from the ocean. There was a swimming pool in the back and a lot of ghosts of old movie stars. Sometimes in the night we heard them out there partying and laughing around the pool. Things were good. The Last Chances were about to cut another record. Getting ready for a national tour. And Claudie was pregnant.

When she found out for certain we all went to Chinatown to celebrate. "But seventeen is too young to be pregnant," Claudie said that night.

Dan told her it would be fun to have a kid to grow up with. And she could keep on working if she wanted to. He'd buy a farm in Texas so we could fly out there and get fresh air and the baby could learn to ride horses and feed chickens. Dan liked chickens. He'd nearly been elected sheriff of Buda, Texas once running on a legalize pot and let chickens run free platform.

That night he got a fortune cookie that said, "You are going to make a significant trip." Mine said, "You will soon play an important role." 'Course we didn't think much about either one at the time.

The next day Claudie was on the back porch working on her glass paintings, little glass squares she put together with flowers and leaves in the middle. She was selling them in a store the Moonies ran over on Santa Monica Boulevard. I was always afraid the Moonies were going to kidnap her 'cause they kept coming to the house and talking about the condition of the world. I told them our condition was pretty good. If they were worried about conditions they oughta go to West Virginia. Sometimes Zook would start drumming or vacuuming till it drove them out.

Dan and Zook were gone to the Watts Towers, those crazy towers Simon Rodia worked on for thirty-three years and then walked off and left one day after people made fun of them. Dan thought it was a spiritual place. He'd put three blue willow plates over our front door, like Simon Rodia had over his. Late in the afternoon Zook phoned crying, saying for us to come to UCLA Medical Center. Dan had been shot.

When we got there Zook was waiting outside the emergency room. Between crying and hiccups he told us what happened. They'd been returning from Watts and somewhere around La Brea Avenue they'd seen an accident, not even a real bad accident. But Dan pulled the van over to see if anybody needed help. He walked up to a car and the other driver jumped out and started blowing people away. Dan got hit in the stomach. The man blasted everyone he could see and then took off.

We waited. Merle always said places develop their own grief. Prison is like that, walls hold the misery. You can feel it. This room was like that. There was a bright orange line down the length of the corridor and around the side of the room. We walked up and down the orange line. Zook drummed his fingers. Claudie smoked. I drank Dr. Peppers.

We waited. When the doctor finally came out he talked for a while before we could figure out what he was saying.

Dan was alive, he said, but there was spinal injury. Part of him was dead.

When we got back to the house Claudie broke her glass pictures and cut her arms lengthwise like the orange line that ran down the corridor of the hospital.

She was all right after a few days but it was all ghosts from there. Real quiet ones. No music. No parties. The gold was gone. In UCLA Medical Center Dan lay there turning the color of the sheets. Even the red beard started to dim.

The group split. Most of them back to San Francisco. Claudie and I got a couple of rooms not far from the hospital. I went to work at an Instant Taco stand on Wilshire. Every day I'd see Dan. "Goddamn fucking madness to go through Vietnam and end up like this," he said one day. But most days he'd cheer me up. His plan was that as soon as he could sit up he'd play the fiddle till they threw him out. It was the hospital that was fucking him up, he claimed. He'd be all right, if they'd just let him alone. I got the feeling he thought if he could just get outta that building and that Mr. Clean madness around him he could sprout wings if he wanted to and heal himself.

Meanwhile Claudie went into healing. Went to churches and lighted candles. Communed with priests and faith healers and Zen Buddhists and gypsy spiritualists and voodoos who did things like put chicken feet and candles around the floor.

One night she came home in the middle of the night. She'd been getting some strong stuff and that night she was coming down from a high and just about crawling on the floor. So she crawled into my bed saying she was scared to be alone. I got up and found us a bottle of rum and a couple of Penwalt twenty-mill Biphetamines. I knew what she wanted. She wanted a comforting body. Like some kid that has fallen down and torn her dress and skinned her knees runs home to mama.

Merle used to say to me, "Oh, Tennessee, just think of all the loves you have ahead of you, son," and I'd say, "Merle, let's just talk about toothaches," 'cause what she was talking about had been going on in the next bed all my life and I could do without it. I'd grown up with it along with black eyes and bruised jaws and screaming in the night. My all time favorite love of Merle's turned a shotgun on both of us one day after spraying the other side of the room and out the window with buckshot and held us there all afternoon till it got dark enough for the cops to come up and shoot him through the window.

And some of those same friendly loves might even take an interest in a kid home from school with chicken pox. Or sitting in a movie, slide fingers greasy from popcorn into the fly of the kid beside him he's supposed to be taking care of. So before I was old enough to know the words for it I was already saying, oh, no, not that again.

So, okay, maybe somewhere in the dark with a good high and a lot of loud music and somebody who's gonna split the next minute so there's never the light of day or anything to say. But in my book you didn't crawl into bed with someone you cared about. Surely not like I cared about Claudie. And Dan. The very thought put me on a freak. So

I just sat there in bed beside her and talked and turned on some music and rubbed her back till she went to sleep.

Things went on at a steady down and brown. There were circles under Claudie's eyes and her hair didn't always smell like honeysuckle hair rinse anymore. I wanted to push all the trouble out of her mind, which was just what the coming-on movie writer was doing, introducing her to new things to keep her mind off Dan so pretty soon her head was hitting the ceiling all the time.

So one night I told her she better jump off the merrry-go-round before it was riding her. I told her she was giving up too soon. The first time we ever met, the first words she ever said to me, I reminded her, was that Dan was magic, right? And I said, besides that she oughta be thinking about the baby now.

I threw a heavy trip on her. And she started crying. So I tried to lighten it up by going into a West Virginia sermon. "One of these days, Claudie girl, the Lord's gonna look down here and see if you and me is on the side of the angels, smiling and singing and cutting out paper dolls . . ." talking silly till I made her laugh. And she came over and hugged me and said, "I love you, Tennessee," and I think she did.

But one day not long afterwards she was gone. She left a note saying she was going on location to Hawaii with a film crew and would be back in a few weeks.

In about a week I got a letter:

> *Think of the most beautiful music you ever heard, Tennessee, the best fiddle Dan ever played, and that is*

Hawaii. I don't expect to find a more beautiful world outside heaven.

All the old Hawaiian gods are still here. When we first arrived I was trying to make some rubbings of a prehistoric fish etching in the petroglyph fields where the wind blows all the time and the Pacific below the cliffs is blinding blue. And while I was there, kneeling on the ground, I saw the Imarchers, the old Hawaiian gods. You are supposed to die if you see these gods in their feather capes and Otheriian helmets, but I didn't. They went off up the pali; *the next day Pele sent a lava flow down the Imarchers' exact path. No doubt they were trying to warn me.*

I told them we should film that.

We have been camping at Hapuna Beach and shooting background and collecting psilocybin mushrooms. There are three varieties here just like in Mexico.

I don't know how long we'll be here. There's talk we might move on to Mexico. I'd as soon stay here awhile, but it doesn't matter. What matters, Tennessee?

I feel fine. I'm getting bigger. I wish you were here. I miss you.

Write me about Dan. I think of him and think of him and think of him. He is a constant shadow in my heart. Will he ever forgive me for going off? I love him. He knows that doesn't he, Tenn? And you.

Claudie

I wrote back that Merle told me never to cross water except on a bridge 'cause Aunt Lollie drowned in the South

*Branch of the Potomac when she was sixteen and Cousin
Deedie, Merle's first cousin twice removed and her little girl
Sonja (for Sonja Henie, Merle said) both drowned in a pond
outside Wolf Summit, West Virginia, in 1950 with her
husband just stationed in Georgia where he ran off AWOL
in grief because of Cousin Deedie, though they weren't
getting on anyway and Sonja—the little girl—wasn't his
little girl. And Aunt Girl (she was always called that) had a
husband whose brother drowned in a U.S. Navy submarine
in the Indian Ocean.*

*And I sent her a song: "Culver City Is Blue Without
You."*

Culver City is blue without you,
All the palm trees quit waving,
All the surf has stopped breaking,
The surf boards have drowned in the ocean

Claudie, it's blue without you,
On the corner men are crying,
All the birds are just dying,
Without you to sing to.

The streetlights don't shine as bright as before,
The freeways don't lead to no place no more

Culver City is lonely without you,
The movies quit making
The go-go girls quit shaking
The moon's always blue without you, without you.

It is such an obvious "nest," the townhouse Maureen
and Grey share—living in sin, he thinks, harkening back
to his Methodist grandmother's phrase. It is chic and
expensive, located near the State Department and Watergate. From the outside it looks hardly big enough for a
bathtub. Unfortunately it is big enough for an entire
household including a bed. Still, George feels like a
buffalo standing before the neat, aged wood door with the
shutters and the geraniums in the window box, the entire
width of the house hardly wider than he could reach.

Grey likes grass, Maureen said to explain it instead of
an apartment.

Ah, yes, Grey likes grass! Poetic.

The kind you walk on, she added before he could. The
other kind too, she'd let him know. Grey was up to the
minute in everything.

Time was, he thinks, looking at the dark streets, when she'd have been afraid to live here. When she was his she was afraid. But then she never was *his*, he had to remember that. It is part of his readjustment or enlightenment or coping, what have you. It was just that kind of thinking that caused the trouble, she claimed, the world claimed.

He sees the light in the peephole after ringing the bell.

"Who is it?" she calls.

"The ice man."

"George, you weary me!"

"'I think that I shall never see a poem lovely as a tree.' Is that the password?" Cut it out, he tells himself, or you'll never get in. "Do I have to stand out here and shout?"

There's a noisy bit of latching and unlatching and the door opens two and a half inches. He can see the pink nose and partial whiskers of his former cat Caesar come to inspect the stranger at the door.

"I came to apologize," he says sincerely, or *trying* to be sincere. He was sincere when he decided to come. It was the "nest" and the arrogant white cat that shook his pure intentions.

She sighs, never believing him well-intentioned. "Don't let Caesar out," she directs.

He enters with a bottle of Chivas Regal under his arm. "How's the first immortal cat?" he asks patting Caesar, whom he never liked. The feeling was mutual.

"Happy anniversary," he says, extending the bottle he's brought.

"Oh, come on, George, not again. And why not just ask for a drink?"

"I don't want to put you out, Maureen. Impose on Grey."

She made a face of exasperation. It wasn't their anniversary but he always said that since it was such an obvious jar. Even *ex*-wives were sensitive about anniversaries.

"Let's be friends," he says nicely. He sets the bottle on the round glass cocktail table set on the white furry rug set on the elegant oriental. He allows himself one glance around the room to see if anything is out of order. It isn't. Casual elegance. Lots of hardbound books. The tiny pieces of antique furniture she and Grey "enjoy" are settled about the room like jewels to dare the barbarian intruder. She wasn't even watching TV but reading a book, a thick book calling up the unquiet spirits of women artists who've been ignored through the centuries. There are no magazines or newspapers and no unchic vice he can catch her at.

She brings him a glass of ice and a small pitcher of water and a bright red drink for herself which looks to him like Kool-Aid.

"What's that?"

"Campari and soda."

"I'm sorry," he says, knowing it annoys her when he apologizes and over trifles.

Caesar has returned to his curled position on the white furry rug at Maureen's feet. They look like a portrait.

"Have you ever thought of using Caesar on your program? He could crouch on your shoulder and add an air of mystery. He's getting fat," he adds.

"You always say that."

"He is."

"Well, he's old, he has a right to get fat."

"That's what I tell myself." He drank half the glass of scotch poured over Maureen's bottled ice cubes.

"How have you been? Since Texas, I mean?"

"All right," she says. She does not want to discuss it. Clearly. She tilts her head in her judging posture with her knees pulled up protectively before her on the couch as if she anticipates attack. It occurs to him that under the law he could probably get away with it. She is his wife still. And she is living with another man. In the South not long ago he could shoot them both and get away with it. He drinks a minute quietly.

"What do you think of me, Maureen? Pretend you're assigned to do a story on your ex-husband, explaining him to the rest of the world. Tell me this and I'll never bother you again."

He looks for a smile. "You'll bother me again, and you really don't want to know what I think."

"Oh, I do, with all my heart and soul and nostrils."

There is some hint of a smile now. She is nice tonight, he thinks, nice and patient. They switch back and forth being nice and patient. Or at least they used to. Now she's usually nice and patient and he's usually neither. Gracious, she is, when she has every right to be definitively angry.

"Are you still mad?" he asks her.

"Would you be?"

"You forget I taught you that—responding with a question to evade the answer."

"Serves you right," she says and turns her head in exasperation the way she used to do talking to Claudie sometimes. He sees everything with her through layers, like sheer curtains of the past.

"George, I can't talk to you. Never. I guess I never could talk to you. You don't talk straight."

"You know, that's what I've been thinking about everyone else."

"See what I mean." She lifts her hands in a very Italian gesture. It reminds him that she and Grey went to Italy the past summer. Poets and lovers. How nice it must have been holding hands and walking down the Spanish Steps. Screwing in Venice while the water lapped outside.

He looks down and finds some unidentifiable stain on his brown pants. When he lifts his drink the coaster stays with it an instant and then clatters loudly back on the glass table.

"I'm sorry about the other day," he says again. "I'll give you a divorce. I think you and Grey should get married and live happily ever after. I'm all for it."

She waits to see what mischief he is leading up to, tolerating him like a boy.

"We're more interesting with one another now, Maureen, aren't we?"

"I don't know," she says.

"We have something to talk about. For years we had

nothing in common but Claudie. Besides I like you more,"
he says. "Have I told you I admire what you're doing? It's
good what women are doing. It was time. If it had come
sooner Claudie might have stayed at home. Don't you
agree?" he asks, knowing he is putting her in an
impossible position. She has to agree with his woman
stand and on the other hand she will never discuss
Claudie. Never.

"There's no use in discussing what might have been."

"If I had been different then," he says.

"Stop it," she says coldly, "I don't want to talk about
that."

He looks at her, her eyes stern, her face set hard, and
wonders at the strength she had bottled inside her all those
years he knew her. He wonders sometimes what he really
thought of her during those years. Now he isn't sure. He
was content with her but hardly conscious of her most of
the time as separate from the motions she made—those
that irritated him and those that he took for granted. But
surely it wasn't that simple. Now he'd probably never
know unless he were hypnotized and taken back in time.

"Maureen, tell me if I'm a foolish, helpless, unemployed . . . ," he looks for a word to complete the list and
finally settles for "male?"

"You're no fool. You mismanage." She says it lightly,
unafraid and casual.

"Why mismanage?"

She sighs now, willing to watch him but not willing to
put enough of herself in to participate in the ritual.

"Quit the torture," she says kindly.

"I appreciate your talking to me, Maureen. My confidants are fewer and older these days."

"Why don't you talk to Elizabeth?"

"Oh, I do, but there's just so much I can say, you know. That's the difference, isn't it? You can talk yourself down to a wife but to a lover you have to hold your shoulders back, don't you? Or at least that's the way it seems to work."

She smiles acknowledging some truth but unwilling to go all the way. "I'm not getting into this, George. I don't think we actually have all that much to talk about."

"We have more to talk about with one another than any other people we know."

"What a pity then, if it's true," she says.

"What do you and Grey talk about? Poetry?"

She stands then and he knows it is going badly and will go down from then on. It is always just a matter of when the glass will turn and the sand start running the other way.

It takes enormous effort to pull himself up, as if he's actually lifting the roof of the little house. "Okay," he says. "It's okay about the divorce. Whatever you want."

He turns and goes to the door bumping into a small round table that probably arrived on the *Mayflower*. "God, this is a little place," he says. He turns back then, and his dignity already shaken, he goes back to the glass cocktail table and picks up the Chivas Regal and puts it under his coat.

"It is too late for empty gestures of magnanimity, isn't it? I'm sure Grey drinks fermented French hummingbird juice anyway." He sounds drunk and wonders why when he hasn't drunk enough for that. A psychological drunk. Sure sign of deterioration. A futile and immature plea for sympathy. She unlatches the chain and steps back, obviously relieved he is leaving without a worse scene.

He pulls his shoulders to attention and touches the cat in Maureen's arms. Caesar blinks and then yawns luxuriously casting an odor of fish into the air.

"By the way, there's a weird kid around who claims he knew Claudie, saw her right before she died. Don't be surprised if he drops out of a tree on you one day."

"I'll be prepared," she says, offering in her eagerness for him to leave, as short a reply as possible. He starts to add something more about Tennessee when her phone rings.

"Well, best to Grey," he says, but the door is already closed.

In the back of the bus, hugging the Chivas Regal under his jacket he pretends to be oblivious to the teenage dudes in front of him casting mocking glances his way. One is a small kid with a narrow face under a red velvet slouch hat. Elizabeth would love it, having a penchant for extravagance of that sort. And it makes him smile, the absurdity, the splendid fantasy life required to wear such a hat on the dirty-windowed, listing bus which just happens to be passing the White House. And suddenly the kid reminds him of a poet who read the night he first set eyes on Grey.

Grey was no closet poet. He gave occasional readings, even at the Folger Shakespeare Library, where the nation's literary cream regularly rose. Though George had noticed announcements of Grey's readings in the local newspapers he had never been able to bring himself to observe Grey in a pristine, brightly lighted hall of sober-minded poetry admirers. But one day walking down the street he passed a bar with a chalkboard announcement outside. Poetry reading tonight! Three names. Grey's first. The idea haunted him all day. Over a beer it might be tolerable. He was maddeningly curious. And what else had he to do. It was before he'd met Elizabeth.

That night he elbowed his way to the bar feeling as appropriate as a palm tree in the midst of the stringy bodies and serious faces. Maureen was at a round table by the window, smoking. Comfortable. No palm tree. And there was Grey, his poetry books in front of him, thin, gold-rimmed glasses, hair slightly long, slightly balding, enough to denote sexual prowess without being unattractive. A tweed jacket with patched elbows, the hip, academic and poet. Right. Together. A man who would never have hemorrhoids or buy *People* magazine.

They were talking to another man, laughing, animated. Sound equipment was being installed. The readings would be recorded. George stared at them until Maureen, glancing around the bar, saw him. She offered the slightest nod with no smile attached. He considered escape just as his beer arrived. The kid in the red velvet slouch hat took the stool behind the microphone and began to read about brothers and the womb of Africa, with an occasional Swahili chant thrown in.

When Grey arose there was applause and an eager stirring throughout the room. Then the slim voice, a bit rough, rich, began to read. He read poems with spare, simple words that George, so distracted by the presence of the man, nevertheless couldn't follow. Once his eyes fell on George and lingered. Did he recognize him from some picture of Maureen's? Did he simply wonder at the odd man in support socks, sweating without understanding in the warm, smoky bar?

He read a poem dedicated to Maureen.

Across from me
Your hand on my knee
Each other and no other
A day alone . . .

George turned to Maureen. She was not watching Grey but resting her chin on her hands, looking down. There was something prayerlike in her manner, peaceful in the restfulness of her shoulders. He knew then that she had found something he had never given her, something that he could not with certainty even name.

At his bus stop he expects the three dudes to follow him. Maybe they were the ones who'd mugged him before. Taken a contract on him put out by Tennessee Blue—his life and wallet for three songs. But the bus pulls away and they wave at him, laughing, knowing his fears, joyous in their small strength.

He takes a seat on a bench in a small park wrested from an intersection near the great cavern in the middle of the street. There is a workers' strike now. The hole might be there forever until cars fall in over and over and finally fill it with metal. People pass, heading up M Street to the restaurants and bars, to the sidewalk cafes at the end of the block. He drinks from the Chivas Regal. After a while he is joined by a tall, smelly bum who silently sips a bottle of wine. What is the difference between him and me, George wonders, but a place to sleep? George thinks of Grey and Maureen, of Claudie, of the past. When he thinks of the future there is just the gaping hole, construction stopped.

The cop appears out of the blue, all blue, her face navy. "Move on," she says as she approaches. With some dignity the tall, silent bum rises and shuffles off, George watching.

"You, too," the cop says. She is standing before him now. Tall. Authoritative. Young. A sign of growing old, someone said, when cops start looking young. That was even before there were amazon cops.

"I'm a taxpaying citizen," George says, "enjoying the night."

"Don't matter what you are, mister. Move on. Don't give me trouble."

"You're mistaking me for a bum." George pulls the Chivas Regal from under his coat. "Bums do not drink Chivas Regal."

The cop hardly glances at it. It is clearly all Wild Irish Rose to her.

George pulls himself up, feeling a swaying earthquake-like sensation. "I want to get the facts straight. I'm a taxpaying citizen. Currently unemployed," he adds. "Every day I don my aftershave and set out on the great job hunt. It is not Africa but it is a hunt. Alone. Without carriers or guides. I'll bet you can still smell my Old Spice."

As he moves toward her she reaches for her billy club. George stops. She is wearing Indian turquoise earrings. She is also detaching her walky-talky.

George reaches for his billfold and identification. It is not in his back pocket. Or in his right. "My billfold's been stolen," he shouts. He remembers a lurch of the bus, the three dudes laughing. "I want to report, officer, that my billfold has been stolen."

The cop tilts her head skeptically. An earring swings slowly. George remembers then that his billfold was stolen last week when he was mugged. His money is wadded in his right pants pocket. He tries to explain to the cop who is now lifting the ear of her walky-talky.

Pull yourself together, George. Now is the time for all good men to come to the aid of their country! He takes a deep breath and speaks in his best learned bureaucratic voice. "Officer, I live right around the corner." He mentions the address, which is proper, no flea bag, he points out. "So I'll be going now."

He divines some glimmer of smile about the navy blue face and red lips. She pushes the antenna back into the walky-talky.

"Merry Christmas," George calls. When he looks back at the corner the cop is walking in the other direction. She has a nice figure, George notices.

As soon as the elevator doors open he hears the music from his apartment, slow and odd and electric—booming and loud. It is a general assault as he walks toward the door.

They don't hear him until he is inside, has turned the dead bolt, hung his coat, walked down the desecrated hall and is standing before them. When they look up they smile innocently, then he watches their expressions change as they read his face and realize a terrorist has invaded their space. Meanwhile he provides himself with a summary of categories—blundering estranged husband, recent victim of the world's abused chosen randomly in a dark alley, incipient bum, transient boarder and lover. One who does not abide. It is maybe the way Claudie felt a million times, never fitting the appointed glass slipper.

Suddenly there is spontaneous combustion of the Chivas Regal within him. The music stops in mid-blast. Tennessee is rising cross-legged from the floor and he hears himself muttering curses. He grabs for Tennessee's arm, catches only a handful of shirt, then swings with his right arm and smashes Tennessee in the face, his knuckles square on the cheek bone so that he feels the pain in his hand as he watches Tennessee fall back slowly, pulling the organ with his foot so that he and the chord organ crash in a great cacophonous roar that accompanies Elizabeth's cry.

For a moment George stares at Tennessee on the floor as if he weren't sure himself why Tennessee is there looking up at him, his hard, West Virginia face ironed with the blow he's received. But Tennessee recovers fast—*as a young man*—and he rises, glancing around the room in the manner of those knowing and vulnerable, looking for additional force. And then Tennessee catches himself and stops. He stares at George seeing something he's been looking, maybe reluctantly, to find. His hands drop to his sides and his body slumps.

"Man, you ain't worth the trip," Tennessee says, staring at George in his hard, cheap way.

He turns away, wiping blood from his mouth onto his jeans. He unplugs the chord organ and winds the cord. Elizabeth brings him a damp washcloth, a new one George notices, velvety blue like the cop in the park. Tennessee presses the cloth to his mouth a moment, then tosses it onto the coffee table. He picks up his chord organ and his notebook.

"I leave my worldly possessions," he says, raising one hand and proclaiming toward the kitchen, "to the indomitable man." He offers Elizabeth an apologetic shrug.

George listens to the retreat of Tennessee's yellow boots down the hall. He lifts the washcloth off the wood coffee table. He begins to speak before he turns to face Elizabeth.

"If I hadn't done something . . .," he begins, "he would have been here . . .," he gestures holding the washcloth, "for forty years . . ."

Elizabeth is lighting one cigarette and stubbing out another. She dips her head in a gesture of slight affectation that he has always admired inordinately. Then she looks at him as she would at some stranger across a desk, someone to analyze and designate as a non-head of household without children, family, job or toilet of one's own. She folds her thin arms, barring him in vivid body language.

"You made a mistake," she says. "Tennessee came here for a very good reason. He told me tonight that Claudie had a baby."

A baby. For a moment he's not sure what it means. A *baby*, as if the word itself were unfamiliar.

"A baby?" he says.

"The baby is Tennessee's responsibility. He came to see if you would take care of it."

Feeling as if he were drugged he watches Elizabeth move about the room, angry as he has never seen her, telling him that Tennessee came to him rather than Maureen because he'd helped them once before. And somehow he believed Claudie had told him to find her father.

"Of course, he wasn't expecting to run into the Green Berets!" she says finally.

She takes a drag on the cigarette and stubs it halfway out. Then without looking at him again she goes into the bedroom, leaving a thin, slow ribbon of smoke trailing after her.

Immediately he thinks to run after Tennessee, hold him, capture him. But he would be gone by now. So he sags into a chair, letting the idea jell in his mind. A baby.

Later in bed, their backs turned to one another: "Why didn't he tell me earlier? Why didn't they tell me when she died and I was there? Babies don't just get lost!"

She leaves the question empty as though the dark alone will take care of it and he is thinking, of course, babies get lost and children get lost, anyone can get lost along the way.

"What did he say? Exactly?"

"That Claudie had a baby. That he was Claudie's friend."

"Boy friend? The father?"

"'Friend' was the word he used."

"That's all he said?"

"Yes."

"Why didn't he just come and tell me? Just straight-away like normal people?"

She sighs. They have argued before about his defini-tion of "normal." To him "normal" is simply what *he* would do, she claims.

"What right has he to check me out?"

"He wanted to know you. Would you trust *him* just by looking at him?"

George groans.

He tries to imagine Claudie's baby. He hasn't seen a baby in a long time to really notice. Sometimes a baby in the supermarket would give him pause, especially the beautiful black babies with their dark water eyes. He can hardly remember Claudie as a baby. That time seemed to fly by so quickly, leaving a few snapshots, and memories.

"What will you do?" she asks him, turning in the bed touching his shoulder by accident but not moving away.

"I'll talk to him."

"But what if he doesn't come back?"

Of course, that was what he had been trying to do, run him off. "I'll find him. I'll find the baby."

"Then you and Maureen would have something to share."

"Yes," he says, thinking how strange that would be and how surprising for Elizabeth to mention it. The idea that she might worry about his feelings toward Maureen is new.

"And you? How would you feel about it?" he asks her.

"I don't know. I'd have to wait and see."

Her reply was more than reasonable. "You're honest, Elizabeth."

"I know. And you think that's a virtue."

"Yes." It has never occurred to him that it might not be.

He tried to place Claudie with Tennessee, then as a woman and a mother. For this he sees her differently. Mothers look so young nowadays. Is it possible she was a mother? It is the first peaceful thought of her he's had in months. A mother. There must have been something good with that.

He lies in the dark thinking of a child, trying to

imagine it, and a kind of excitement grows in him, a sense of possibilities beyond a new job or a million dollars.

The faint hum of the electric clock stops and they are left in silence. The power has been shut off again. It happens often and mysteriously in the night. Sometimes it is accompanied by a loud electrical hum from the street, some subtle, alien torture of the populace. It begins suddenly now and George curses and turns in the bed trying to cover his ears with his pillow.

"Spacemen have taken over the telephone company again."

She doesn't reply. There is nothing but the hum which is penetrating his body and pressing on his most sensitive nerves. The world directed by a mad dentist.

"God, I've fucked up!" he says into the darkness.

"Fucked-up isn't usually terminal," Elizabeth says.

"I have to find the baby, Elizabeth."

"You will, George," she says softly.

The buzz stops suddenly and the familiar hum of the clock resumes.

He sits up, phones Time and resets the clock.

"I love you, Elizabeth," he says when he lies back down.

"Goodnight, George," she says.

I screwed up good, Claudie. Really topped the charts that time. Now he'll know about the kid. No telling what he'll do. Call the FBI. Organize a commando unit. Come hunting his possession for sure. That is if he even believes it. But he won't know the story now unless he gets to heaven and hears it from you or another angel. And you missed out on some of it, Claudie, while you were in Hawaii those weeks. When every musician in the world started plowing into the hospital at all hours, stoned and bearing gifts, beer and grass and enough milligrams of whatever to dry up every mouth in Culver City. Anything they could think of to cheer Dan up. A big red rooster in a cage that started crowing at 4:30 in the morning. A four-foot king snake that Dan put into his bed so that when the nurse pulled back the sheet she did a backward half gainer into the hall.

I got him a cassette player with a headset so he could listen to music while the men in his ward watched TV game shows. The men liked to watch the emcees kiss the women contestants.

Dan claimed the black and white tiles of the hospital floor represented the patients who lived and died. Sometimes he said he watched a white one turn. Down a wing was a whole section of people on machines, human pot plants. One man had been there thirty-four years.

For sport Dan caught flies in a wine bottle.

Then one melody blue day in the great state of California someone stole his fiddle. He rang bells and jerked cords as soon as he discovered it but there was no use. No honor amongst the maimed, he said.

Someone sent him pornographic crossword puzzles. Zook sent him Wonder Wart Hog comics. He got occasional letters from Claudie. Then one day he asked me for her address.

Two weeks later she phoned from the airport. "Tennessee?" she said, and all of a sudden the room was like a home again. She wanted to know if I'd be there for a while. I told her I'd be there till the hen crows and the mud blows. I waited at the window watching the cars on Sunset Boulevard and her song came to be all at once . . .

When the blues are winning and the doors open in
When the sky is falling and you need a friend
If the San Andreas faults and all the oceans halt
Whatever happens, girl, I'll be right here,
      remembering the good times

Oh, Claudie, there is nothing that I wouldn't do
       for you
I'd take a trip to Mars and bring you back a star
Claudie, when your dreams run down I'll wind
       them up again
Whatever happens, girl, I'll be around

She looked better than angels, I told her. Her skin was like caramel and she still didn't look very pregnant. She handed me Dan's letter. The envelope was covered with an ink drawing of a bearded, reclining man riding a wave.

"How you, Claudie? I'm hankering for bluebonnets of late, just lying here thinking about 'em sprouting up about now on the Texas tundra and nodding as the Cadillacs go by. So I just about decided to go back to Texas. I'm just a growing boy and missing the sunshine. And without a smoke in months! They don't take to that kind of thing in here. In fact I'm just lying here rusting away like an old car when you know damn well I oughta be out spinning and raising hell and not just letting the sands of time blow over me.

"Only it's not everybody you can call on to transport a heavy, hairy body across country. Greyhound and May-flower won't handle it. And I know I have a lot of friends but it isn't the same. You know what I mean? So I'm calling on you. I think Tennessee will help. It will take two people. I hate to ask you, Claudie, but please. Dan."

She was watching me read the letter. Holding her breath. I told her, hell, why not. I was getting sick of L.A., why ever' now and then it made me vomit. And that was

113

about the truth. A little bit of instant tacos goes a long way.

She told me she felt awful that she'd gone off but she was okay now, clean. She had her head back on, she said.

I told her everyone's entitled to one stumble when the floor falls in.

So we made plans. Between us we had twenty-three dollars and forty-seven cents. We couldn't get to Santa Monica on that. So every day I'd march off to the Instant Taco stand . . . sauce, lettuce, onion, cheese. Sauce, lettuce, onion, cheese. Sauce, lettuce, onion, cheese . . .

Claudie got a job at an amusement park wearing a Minnie Mouse head. It was a crummy job.

A man offered her a hundred and fifty dollars to play house with Minnie Mouse.

Finally she decided to write her father for money and George Perry sent more than she'd asked for. I couldn't get over it. That's when I got the idea that George Perry might be a sort you could share your tent with.

So after trying fourteen used car places, at Tom Tom's Used Cars—Tom in an Indian war bonnet—I found a man with maroon patent boots who said he could find us wheels. Zook had the van and Dan's old Plymouth wouldn't make Pasadena. The car was a light blue Thunderbird in Glendale in a garage with two others bandaged up and fresh painted.

"It looks like a movie star," Claudie said, both of us wishing for something quieter.

"You get to Houston you phone Better Used Cars and ask for Clark," said the man in the maroon patent shoes.

"That's C-L-A-R-K, Clark. Clark will be expecting you in less than a week." He leaned forward, his mirrored sun glasses cutting into his face like headlights. "Now I want to especially emphasize that they gonna be expectin' you to arrive. And if you don't arrive before that week is up they gonna come lookin' for you. And if they come lookin' for you, son, they gonna find you. And them cats play rough ball. It wouldn't be much fun. Wouldn't leave much hangin'."

"Happy trails," he said.

Interstate 10 runs from L.A. into the heart of Texas. Stars at night, all that, Dan said. "Just get onto Interstate 10 and don't stop till we hit Austin."

He'd been moved from the hospital to the overflow house across the street. Body storage depot, he called it. He was waiting on the front porch with a smile like a flag waving when we drove up. We wheeled him to the car with an orderly hollering that Dan was crazy. What did he think he was doing! He couldn't even pee!

We got him into the back seat of the Thunderbird and took off. Claudie driving. Dan rolled down his window and let the air blow on his face.

"California, I don't hate to see you go," he said. He looked out the window a few miles, his face so ragged with relief, I looked away. After a while he went to sleep. When he woke he wanted a smoke and a bottle of wine. Then he began singing "Oh, Lord won't you buy me a Mercedes

Benz" and we sang along and he began talking about how wonderful it was gonna be when we hit Texas. He had friends with a houseboat on Lake Travis. We'd get a place out there, maybe. They were making movies in Austin. Claudie could work. Lots of music, too, Tennessee, he said. "We'll reassemble the Last Chances, get the sound and start again! When the baby comes we'll be all set up," he kept saying. We'd love it. Have a few chickens, tomato plants, a little grass growing for diversion.

We drove to Blythe that night and stopped in one of the first motels in Arizona. It was all we could do to get him out of the car and inside to the bed.

He seemed okay at first with Claudie lying down beside him, he even got to feel the baby kick, but he couldn't sleep. When he'd fall off to sleep a minute he'd groan. By the next afternoon he was out of his head with fever and talking about snakes. He said after a storm in West Texas rattlesnakes come out to sun themselves on the roads and sometimes wrap around the wheel of a car so when you get out to change a tire or even buy gas, it's zap, you're dead.

When we got to Tucson we drove straight to a hospital. Claudie and I spent the night in the waiting room.

The next morning the doctor didn't want Dan to leave. He said people in his condition are subject to infections in the lower intestinal tract. He should stay there until the fever is gone and the infection is checked, he said. He took no responsibility whatever if Dan left.

We were in a small white room with Muzak seeping out of the acoustical tiles.

"Like fuck we're gonna stay here," Dan said. "Hell,

we're nearly to Texas. I'm not stayin' here!"

I imagine they heard him all over the hospital. Claudie threw her blue denim bag over her shoulder and leaned against the wall. She looked worn out and ready to cry.

Dan said we might never get there if we stopped now. "Hell, woman, that kid is gonna be born in Texas!" He was shouting and at the same time lying there so flat his body looked like it was nailed down at the corners.

I was afraid to leave but I knew we'd end up doing what he wanted us to do. And of course we did. We got some medicine and left.

By afternoon Claudie was going to sleep at the wheel so I drove. She said all I had to do was just sit there and hold the car in the road. Nothing to it, she said. Just like playing cars.

The land was like an omen. Empty. Sand and sky. Sometimes a fence. Heat brought up ghosts on the highway. For miles we wouldn't see another car. I kept turning on the radio to make sure everybody else hadn't been killed by the bomb. I wouldn't have been surprised to see chariots rolling out of heaven announcing the end of the world.

Dan was half the time burning or freezing. He dreamed he was a wooden egg with no legs. When we stopped for coffee in El Paso I woke him up to say we were in Texas and he said he knew 'cause there was a monster in a pickup following us and every time he was in Texas that monster followed him around.

The cashier in the Dairy Queen said it was a good twelve-hour drive into Austin.

Outside Van Horn I was driving again. Claudie was

sleeping and Dan was passed out or sleeping, we couldn't tell by then. I turned on the radio to keep awake and found a friendly deejay that sounded like West Virginia. But the news was all Texas: A damaged oil tanker blocked the Houston ship channel. The governor was accused of absenteeism. A Dallas policeman had murdered his girl friend. A football coach had resigned. Then the friendly deejay played country gold and I was feeling better, singing along, thinking how music heals the heart and soothes the spirit when I saw the lights come on and a highway patrol car pulling out behind us. Then I knew for sure this wasn't anything at all like playing cars.

The patrol car tailed us for a mile before turning on the red light and pulling us over at Rosie's Twenty-Four Hour Truck Stop. The driver was young. Wore a wide-brimmed brown hat and a tan uniform and a gun on his hip. Real cool-ass type. He took a stroll around the Thunderbird before he came to the window.

"Hi you folks?" he said, like he was the Welcome Wagon.

He asked to see my license and the car registration and shone a flashlight around inside the car, waking Dan into a cursing fit. I told the patrolman our friend was real sick and we were rushing him home to Austin. He took the keys to the Thunderbird and told me and Claudie to follow him.

Inside Rosie's Twenty-Four Hour Truck Stop the patrolman dusted his hat off and spoke to three farmers in a booth and asked the waitress how she was feeling. He ordered steak and eggs and coffee. The waitress was listening to the same friendly deejay I'd been listening to.

When the patrolman got his coffee he began to tell us how we were in a mighty lot of trouble—his words. First off, driving a stolen vehicle. Driving without a license. He raised his fingers counting along, dunking his eggs in a pool of catsup on his plate. Speeding, driving under the influence of alcohol and other drugs. Crossing the state line for immoral purposes.

"That's five," he said holding up five fingers, "just right off the top of my head, that's five."

Claudie went to the restroom and Jerry Jeff Walker and the Last Gonzos started singing and the patrolman sipped his coffee. He was not as tall as me or as big as Dan. He had a crease across his forehead from the wide-brimmed hat. When he finished his coffee he stabbed his cigarette into the catsup and told me he was gonna go see what he could do for us.

I sat there watching him make calls from the phone booth in the back of the restaurant and listening to Jerry Jeff and the Last Gonzos . . .

Just gettin' by on gettin' by's my stock in trade
Livin' it day to day, pickin' up the pieces wherever
    they fall
Just lettin' it roll, lettin' the high times carry the
    low
Just livin' my life easy come easy go

When Claudie got back she asked me what was gonna happen. I told her there was no telling but we didn't have much choice but to sing along and see.

When we started to leave the patrolman said we were gonna take a little "dee-tour." We moved Dan to the back seat of the patrol car and our gear into the trunk. I saw the patrolman throw the keys to the Thunderbird under the seat and we climbed into the patrol car. A bumpersticker on the sun visor said TAKE TIME FOR TEXAS. The patrolman punched his watch. It was 3:16 A.M.

I counted two cars and four trucks on the road. Dan went to sleep. Claudie smoked. There were a few calls on the radio but the patrolman ignored them. Fifteen minutes later he pulled off the road and told us to get our asses outta there and take our sick friend with us. He said there'd be a Greyhound by in about half an hour and we could flag that down and hightail it back to where we come from.

Claudie blew smoke in his face. The patrolman opened his door and got out.

We sat there a minute. There was nothing outside the car, no lights, no buildings, only an empty highway and probably a hundred thousand rattlesnakes.

I climbed out and asked the patrolman if he'd give me a hand with my friend.

He said, "If you can't pull that pisser outta here boy I'll do it for you a ways up the road."

When I woke up Dan he wanted to know what was going on and where was the Thunderbird. The patrolman was watching us, foot propped on the front bumper. "Like hell I'm gettin' outta here," Dan said. "I'm not going back to L.A."

I saw the patrolman make a slight nervous adjustment to his gun holster. He was young and maybe new to his job and maybe quick to settle disputes. I figured we might all be left there for rattlesnake snacks if we gave him a hard time. I let Claudie argue with Dan and asked the patrolman if I could get our gear out of the trunk.

The patrolman ambled to the back and opened the trunk. I reached in and handed him Claudie's bag. When he turned away I felt around for the jack handle or a wrench, something. I pitched out Dan's duffel bag and felt the jack handle. I grabbed it with both hands and came up swinging. It caught the patrolman in the back of the neck. His hands jerked up and I came back across his head and he went down.

It happened fast so I really didn't think about it. I guess that monster in the pickup truck had sure enough caught up with us. I threw our gear in the trunk and picked up the patrolman's hat and asked Claudie if she could drive. A pair of headlights were coming toward us. Claudie started the patrol car. She could drive but she couldn't quit crying.

I told her the patrolman would be all right.

"He was an asshole," Dan said.

The car gave a friendly honk when it passed us. It was the three farmers from Rosie's Twenty-Four Hour Truck Stop.

Around daylight we ditched the patrol car in an abandoned drive-in movie outside Kerrville. I walked to a gas station and found a Mexican in a red pickup who said he'd give us a ride into town. He helped us get Dan in the back end of the pickup and the next thing I knew we were in San Antonio. It was daylight and about a hundred and fourteen degrees. The nearest sign said "Alamo Suzuki— We conquer Boredom."

We checked into a motel. Dan's fever looked like it was up to volcanic and we'd left the medicine in the Thunderbird. Claudie got some aspirin but he couldn't keep anything down. Dan kept saying don't worry, we're home. Everything's gonna be all right. Be cool. But his eyes were looking like apple jelly.

He told me to go to Austin and find his friends on the houseboat. Warren and Joanne. They had a van and would come and get him. And he even had an aunt in Austin who was a nurse, Dan said. No hospital crud.

So I hitched to Austin. It was like trying to hitch to heaven. Waiting across the shopping mall I might as well have been invisible. The cars were going four hundred miles an hour and my head felt like a short order grill and I knew any minute the Texas Rangers might swoop down on me and it would be the sweet by and by before I could get back to Claudie and Dan.

Finally a professor of romance languages stopped. I told him no, I didn't speak any romance language at all. I was from West Virginia and I wrote songs and I had to get to Austin quick. Pronto, he said. Right, I said, that being the extent of my foreign languages. The professor let me out a couple of miles later at the edge of San Antonio and said *not to miss the LBJ Library while I was in Austin. Then a truck driver—Big Shug on his CB—said he'd be glad to carry me to Austin but first he had to stop for lunch at a barbecue place in San Marcos. Outside San Marcos two kids in a black Buick with a six-pack of beer said they'd take me to Austin and even to the lake in exchange for some grass.*

It took them an hour and a half to find the lake and another hour to find the houseboat. Warren had just left in the van but he'd be back any minute, Joanne said. She gave the kids some grass and went back to stringing beads that Warren would sell on the sidewalk across from the University. She said Warren had a Ph.D. in English but he couldn't get a teaching job and they didn't wanna leave Austin. She was working on her Ph.D. in anthropology.

I sat on a deck chair at the end of the houseboat and waited. Waited through the afternoon and evening. At nine-thirty Warren came back in the van.

We reached San Antonio around eleven. The motel room was unlocked and empty. The air conditioner was running. Claudie's purse was on the bed.

Outside, the swimming pool had a pink outer-space glow from the lights in the water as if any minute monsters might start rising. There was a pay phone standing by the highway with the phone dangling off the hook.

Right away I saw a chair angled away from the others and started toward it feeling like I was walking through the water. I didn't ever want to get there. She was sitting and staring at the great dead eye of the water. When she saw me she caught my hands and started talking real slow and strange.

He'd gotten so much worse, she said. Talking out of his head and trying to fight her when she tried to wash his face. She'd gone to the office and called an ambulance. The motel manager bawled her out for bringing a sick man into the motel.

It seemed years before the ambulance arrived. On the way to the hospital the siren stopped. And then she realized it hadn't.

When they got to the hospital and tried to tell her what she already knew, she couldn't hear. There was a strange, buzzing silence in her head, like death itself.

And did you really expect him to come back, George? Did you expect him to walk through that door, paint-brushes in hand, electric organ buzzing, so you'd be able to say, oh, sorry, kid, and have his blue eyes light and blink with forgiveness? Was anything ever in the world that easy?

In the drugstore flipping through *The New Yorker* for the cartoons, he waits expecting the tall figure to appear outside. But there is no one. No one outside the window, no one behind the paperback rack, no one at the counter stool watching in the mirror, no one. He keeps glancing toward the window until a man begins watching him suspiciously.

Yes, a spy! Russian. Siamese. Take me! George drops

The New Yorker onto the *Newsweek* pile and on his way out, makes a low snort as he passes the well-dressed suspicious man.

To Elizabeth he carefully says nothing about Tennessee for two days. Finally she speaks.

"I don't think he's coming back, George. He found out what he wanted to know."

"But he hasn't finished painting the wall."

She rolls her eyes above her yogurt and sesame seed sundae. He protests. Why is the thought so bizarre? Is finishing something one began so strange? Does nothing begin and normally end anymore?

The next day he finds himself before the Capitol Doughnut Shop which has more than half disappeared. No doughnuts in sight. In two weeks it has been evacuated and torn down. Only rubble remains and that mostly hidden by a fence of assorted doors, assorted as the doughnuts were, tall doors, wide doors, thin doors, short doors, green doors, blue doors, all with secrets and histories. And for a minute the change, the rapid alteration, is so disorienting he considers that he might open each door and find their individual worlds behind them, caught and carried along in the tornado of urban transformation.

Sighing under a sky which seems yellow he wanders across the street to the National Portrait Gallery and down the marble corridor lined with paintings of dead presidents. He passes into the adjoining gallery and follows the corridor to a yellow door with a diamond-shaped cut-out in the middle. Inside are children playing with artful toys. A small blonde girl with long hair, wearing striped overalls, is running up and down a ramp squealing as she crashes into a billowing door of aluminum foil. She is two, maybe, George thinks. Claudie's child would be smaller. Twenty pounds. One arm would carry her.

And what if the child is a lie?

But it is true, he knows. Some words fall truthfully onto the air. The kind of truth that knocks the wind from your body. Like knowing you'll die one day.

He turns away from the bright yellow door and walks away from the sounds of the children, down the quiet corridor, past the paintings and sculptures that he knows reflect his time but which for the most part seem meaningless to him. Through a heavy door he rejoins the city. Before him down the steep stairs the earth is open, ripped deep for the new subway. The red clay innards appear raped and violated. He stands thinking he could swan dive from the top step of the museum and with that one defiant leap descend to the bowels of the earth. But he will not descend. On the contrary he will ascend, explore the earth, search the heavens to find the child. He resolves.

The phone ringing at 8:30 is a jolt. George lifts his head from the pillow and pulls the receiver down to him. Elizabeth, presentable to the world, appears in the doorway as George speaks.

"George? Bud Schumaker."

George grunts, pulls himself up, swings his legs off the bed. "Yeah," he says.

"You sick?"

"Asleep," George says. "It's what the unemployed do. Sleep late. It cuts out a meal. It also keeps us from snarling the rush-hour traffic loitering about."

Bud Schumaker laughs.

"Sorry, but I have to postpone our lunch. How about next week?"

"Sure," George says. And then waking to the world he

remembers Claudie's baby. "Well, actually Bud, I forgot something. I'm not sure about next week. Let me give you a call."

There is a moment of disapproving silence on the other end of the phone.

"Well, sure, sure. Give me a call when you can make it. Don't wait too long." He tried to make the last light but George recognized it as a typical bureaucratic threat. The man couldn't help it. It was compulsive as a tic.

The next sound George hears is a quiet buzz of non-connection. He deposits the phone and looks down at his feet on the burgundy rug beside the bed. They look like dead white fish.

"I left the water on," Elizabeth calls.

"Goodbye," he says. He looks up and is surprised to see her smiling at him wistfully. She crosses the room and kisses him quickly. "Ta," she says.

He hears the apartment door close behind her, a sound he hates. It makes him feel left behind and dreary. Housewives must feel like that every day, he thinks. Or maybe they are grateful to be alone, which could be worse.

He goes to the window and sees the tomato plants across the way are eight inches and listing. Definitely needing water. He waits thinking the girl might come out and water. It is already a hazy day. In the bathroom he can hear the radio in the next apartment stationed to all news and commercials. The President is talking about terrorism. There's been a gay riot in San Francisco.

Passing the refrigerator he sees the last three days' mail on top. The mail is never in the same place twice in this apartment. He swears and screams to himself about the disorder. Outside her work Elizabeth has no regard for routine and habit. She doesn't even use zip codes.

There is a blurb from a men's store announcing a sale, a leftover from employment. And there is his letter to Midstream Employment Consultants, returned. NO LONGER AT THIS ADDRESS. They are probably in Hawaii, Florida, Texas and Arizona, he thinks, having taken their own jobs. He tosses the letter into the wastebasket.

He eats his cereal standing at the kitchen window, pulling dead leaves off Elizabeth's plants and wondering what Claudie's baby is doing at that instant. If the child is well and cared for decently. Today, he swears to himself, he will find Tennessee. He will find Tennessee even if it takes him to New York or Teheran.

He sets the soggy cereal down and moves to the hallway with his coffee and looks at the half-painted drawings—the trees, birds, the man in the corner playing the violin. Suddenly George feels there is something more there. He cradles his coffee and puts his ear to the wall and hears music, a fiddle, peaceful and sweet. It is from the next apartment maybe. But he listens. He turns then and sees that across the street the girl is watering her tomatoes. Suddenly as though he were thirsty and listing, he feels revived. This is it! he says. It will be the greatest job of investigative work since Watergate.

Shortly before noon he is sitting at the dim bar of the

Ben-low Club which is slowly filling with those who prefer to drink their lunch. The manager stands behind the bar eating a submarine sandwich.

"You had a group in here last Sunday, Lost in Space?"

"That's right. Weird. You a cop?"

"Oh, no, I'm just looking for a guy that hangs out with them who might help me reach my daughter. No trouble."

"Well, I got them from Fay. She gets my people. They weren't the most reliable but nobody is anymore. They were so freaky I thought they might catch on, but they were too far out for here. This is an Irish music crowd. Lots of drinking. People don't associate drinking with outer space. That's drugs, you know? But anyway I didn't have to fire them. They just didn't show one night." He takes a bite of the submarine and chews. "Fay was pissed off, I was pissed off. They'd gone out investigating some flying saucer sight. You want Fay's number?"

George follows him up the back stairs into a littered room with a desk and a cot and a blonde Afghan dog spread on the floor.

"Here you go, Scarlett." The dog growls as she finishes the submarine sandwich. The manager rummages. Bills and papers float onto the floor.

"Fay Louise, that's what she calls herself. Tough lady."

George phones from downstairs. "I'm interested in hiring a group," he says.

"Where 'bouts you located?" Fay Louise asks in a bourbon and professional voice.

"Not located yet, but there's a place in the new West End I'm considering."

She is silent a minute. "Well, you call me, mister, when you get started, okay?"

"I'm especially interested in the group called Lost in Space," George says. "I'd like to talk to you." But he's only talking to himself.

The address is across from Malcolm X Park. The doorbell plays a tune. The door opens an inch, chain connected.

"You phoned?" The voice is velvet. He nods. "But you ain't no cop," she says and unlatches the door chain.

"I appreciate that."

"You're probably a Leo. I could tell by looking. And they don't make cops. Ain't suspicious enough. It takes a mean Scorpio like myself to make a cop," she laughs.

The apartment is filled with white furniture with brocaded seats. Through French doors a young man is sunning on a lounge. Fay Louise pours coffee and adds a jigger of brandy to each cup. She is broad and past her prime but beautiful. On the wall over the sofa hangs an enormous portrait of her leaning on a piano.

"Excuse me if I listen to music. I got more audition tapes than hours to listen." She punches a button and the apartment jars with the sound of drums. "Now what you want, honey? I know you ain't opening no clubs any time soon 'cause people like me are moving in before liquor license applications hit the bottom of the in-box."

George asks her about Tennessee and in the process tells her more than he intends.

"Oh, me, kids are a grief, aren't they?" She shakes her head. "I got a son but he hasn't been a free man in five years. That's the worst kinda trouble you can have, trouble with your kid. But I guess I don't have to tell you." She leans forward and touches his hand for an instant and then lifts her coffee cup again.

"I'd like to help you out but all I know is they've left town. Or that's what I was told." She rises and moves toward her desk. "I've seen a lot of crazy black kids but I think white boys win the prize."

The young man on the lounge stirs and turns his body. The music is both drums and chant now.

"From the desk of FAY LOUISE." The address is Takoma Park. "That's where they usually stay. One of them's got family out there. Now don't get carried into outer space," Fay Louise laughs.

The house in Takoma Park is ordinary, a California-style bungalow, painted neatly white, with the sensible symbol of aluminum storm windows and front door. Mrs. Sparachino is a plain woman with dark-owl eyes behind tortoise-framed glasses. She invites him in when he's stated his purpose. He enters a neat, comfortable room with a black leather couch and a fireplace that smells pleasantly of recent use. Over the mantel is a huge photograph which at first glance seems abstract. On closer look George sees it is a stark landscape like a lunar surface but bisected with something like a stone bridge. On another wall is a poster with a quote from a Cornell scientist. *"There has probably been and is at present in the universe an enormous number of life-bearing planets, most of which have evolved an intelligent, technical species . . ."*

"I didn't know anyone had said that."

Mrs. Sparachino smiles at him and he reminds himself that *everything* has probably been said in the course of great blabbering humanity.

"My son and his group have gone to Dallas."

She searches a desk drawer for a minute and hands him a brochure with information about a space association convention. "Here's where they are," she says. "Of course, I can't be sure Tennessee is with them. I know he left with them. They were driving in their van, but the boys are not always predictable," she says smiling. There is a fondness to her tone and George likes her for that.

"How did you get interested in space?"

"I'm a scientist, Mr. Perry. My husband is also. We encountered phenomena in our work for NASA which were unexplainable and troubling."

"And where is this?" he asks, nodding to the photo over the mantel.

"On the moon," she says. "The bridge spans part of a mountain range adjoining Mare Crisium, a large crater. Some people believe that Mare Crisium was once an ocean and this bridge was built to span it."

"Oh," he says. "That's interesting. I didn't . . ."

"Yes. It is endlessly interesting. There's a lot we don't know." She points to a large drawing on another wall. "Actually large areas of the moon are divided into a massive grid system similar to the grid system found on maps. It appears that faults, ridges, rilles and crater chains were laid out in parallel lines intersecting each other at right angles."

Willing to victimize himself again for the sake of curiosity, he asks, "And what happened to the ocean and the grid system?"

Mrs. Sparachino removes her glasses and rubs the bridge of her nose and then looks at George with her large, dark eyes.

"Well, you know Apollo 17 brought back orange glass which didn't relate to the surrounding material."

George nods as if he had known.

"Orange glass is found around nuclear test sites also. Many people believe the orange glass on the moon is evidence of a nuclear explosion. It has been a theory for some years."

"I see," he says. "Thank you very much, Mrs. Sparachino. You've launched me on my way."

By evening he is on a plane for Dallas.

The skies are not so friendly anymore, George thinks, opening the miniature bottle of scotch delivered curtly by an older blonde stewardess wearing a wedding band. He pours the golden liquid over the ice cubes, stirs and looking out the window at the gray and solid emptiness, remembers six months ago, the last and only time he'd flown to Texas.

The call had come straight to his office around noon. He'd often wondered since Claudie left how they'd reach him if anything happened to her. It turned out that such things are done with great efficiency. The sheriff's office in Travis County traced him in less than an hour. He had listened to the simple announcement that his daughter was dead, thanked the caller and had trouble hanging up the phone. All the times he'd feared such a thing, even anticipated it, he was not prepared. He leaned on his desk and tried to steady himself. He lifted his hand and watched it move to the phone. Everything in slow motion. He called Elizabeth. They had only been living together two months. "Oh, no, George!" she said. "I'll meet you at home." Then he phoned Maureen. She was out. So he phoned Grey at the University.

"This is George Perry," he said. "I just got a call from Austin, Texas that Claudie is dead. I can't locate Maureen."

"Oh, God!" he said. "How?"

"I don't know." He could hear typing in the background. He realized he hadn't asked any questions. He, a reporter.

"I'll find her," Grey said simply. "Where will you be?"

George told him he'd check the planes and would be at the apartment. It was a simple and uncomplicated conversation, the first one he'd ever had with the man.

Grey phoned an hour later. "She's here. She wants to go with you. What time are you leaving?"

"There's a four o'clock straight through."

"We'll meet you at the airport. Which one?"

Standing by the great sloping windows of Dulles, he was thinking of Claudie. She was clear to him and real. He could hear her voice, see her almost as if she were there with him but had walked away for a moment. It had been months since she'd phoned. He had asked Elizabeth not to come to the airport. It was easier, he had told her to say goodbye there, though they both knew it was simply awkward with Maureen meeting him.

Grey and Maureen drove up in a small European car. He watched them kiss, a quick familial kiss, but they held on to one another a moment afterward, and watching them he felt for a moment that he had never been part of her life. As though Claudie, too, who had the moment before seemed near and real, were only a dream. As if in the space of time since the phone call from Austin he had lost his past.

Grey left the car in a no-parking zone and carried her bag to the ticket counter. She appeared amazingly composed, a media personage, but then Maureen had never been a crier. George looked away, pretending not to see them but they came straight to his side, utterly civilized, and Grey extended his hand. He looked older in the brightness of day, not so much the graduate student star George had remembered. He was grateful for that. Grey was simply a man. Real. Aging. George knew he wouldn't be able to hate him any longer.

Maureen watched him leave, as much to look at Grey as to not look at him, George knew. "He seems like a nice man, Maureen," he'd said.

Claudie had not been dead twenty-four hours by the time they arrived in Austin—together but separate—stepping out of the plane into a sharp cold wind.

They moved to the rented car—moved, walked, parked, fed their bodies—maddening details, asking men with big hats and women with rough faces where streets were. Austin was a slow, sleepy town with a lot of Latin complexions and a lot of kids wearing jeans. Claudie might have been one of them. A college kid. He kept looking for her everywhere.

"Two singles, please."

The motel man said nothing. Didn't make one quizzical movement even seeing their names the same. Silly, George thought, not to get a double, as if they couldn't be in the same closet and never even realize it. As if their bodies hadn't gone basically deaf and dumb to one another years before.

"Maybe they're wrong," he said to her at one point on the plane. "Sometimes mistakes like that happen."

She didn't reply. She sipped the manhattan, her second, and leaned back and closed her eyes, her mind as remote from him as a cloud out the window.

What was she thinking? he wondered. He couldn't ask. What scene was she seeing? Claudie when? If she'd only tell him what was there in her mind. If she would share her thoughts it would draw him away from his own.

He wanted very much to take her hand. How could they be enemies now?

The next morning they met in the coffee shop. Maureen sat at a counter, something he'd never seen her do. Once she'd have hidden near a window, forever pulling away from where she was. But there she sat at the counter drinking coffee and eating a muffin, the morning sun falling on the soft sheen of unbroken hose on her crossed legs.

He took a seat one down and asked how she'd slept.

"Not too badly," she said, and looked at him, appraising him, a sign of care he'd not expected. And he raised his hand to hide the cut on his chin, knowing she'd read things there he never saw in others because he never took the time to look that closely.

It was too much, being with Maureen, trying to prepare himself for Claudie.

"I don't think you should see her," he told Maureen. But it was he, maybe, who shouldn't have seen.

There was a flash of her naked shoulder under the cloth. A small narrow shoulder. Her hair looked damp and dirty. What's wrong? he kept wondering. Why does she look so awful—so unkempt, so gray?

Her skin was strangely transparent. There was a bruise along her cheek and her nose was swollen. He had not seen her in over two years. She looked different and older. He could truly have said, this is someone I used to know. But there was the jolting reflection of himself in the small bruised face—his mouth, his eyebrows; his same skeptical stare, his coloring. And now she was destroyed. Would decay like a tree.

He turned away then and the man covered her up, straightened the cloth. He had hardly been aware of Maureen there, but seeing her chalky face he took her arm and she allowed it. They walked from the room.

"Is there a restroom?" she asked the large woman at the desk.

He was afraid to let her go, but she pulled away and disappeared down the hall, walking heavily.

The coroner's report: "Look here, I'm a reporter, I know what I can see!" The toughness wasn't necessary.

"You mean for the OD?"

The woman thumbed through a folder and handed him a form familiar from his early days of reporting. How many times he'd read a death summarized tidily on a few lines. And now the inadequate words were swimming before him . . . 2:32 A.M. . . . September 9 . . . acute methamphetamine intoxication . . . accidental . . .

He handed the form back to the woman. "The death certificate . . . ," she was explaining to him . . . "The medical examiner . . ." she pointed down the hall. Her eyes were deep brown waters.

"Let's go," Maureen said.

They began walking down a long glossy floored corridor. There were no windows.

"It was an accident," he said to Maureen. "She didn't intend it."

Afterwards when he felt they should comfort one

another, he went to her room and succeeded in destroying any dignity between them. While the mirror in her makeup case glared at him, Maureen sobbed and he was left alone wondering that she could become so separate. That even then with Claudie dead, she would be separate. He wondered if he had to spend the rest of his life learning again and again the strength of her separation and independence just as he had to learn to live with Claudie's death.

Now, how many hundreds of years later, he is moving toward the same space, the scotch gone, just the small cubes left cooling his hand, the sky dusty. Across the aisle from him and two seats up sits a man with dark diagonal eyebrows that run up his forehead. No one seems to notice him especially except George, who knows immediately he is going the right way. Now all he has to do is follow the man and inevitably he'll find them all—the weird singers and Tennessee and the child and God knows what.

"And what will you do when you find Tennessee?" Elizabeth had asked as he was leaving. She'd been sitting on the bed watching him pack.

"I promise I won't beat him up." He'd tried to make it a joke.

When he'd lifted the phone to call Maureen, Elizabeth had risen to go but he'd caught her arm. So proper she seemed when actually she was careful to protect herself by separating their lives in small, polite ways.

Maureen had answered with her TV voice and he'd known she was not alone.

"Maureen, I have some serious . . ."

"George, this is a bad time," she'd cut him off.

"I'm leaving town in a minute. I need to talk to you." He'd heard his own voice sounding surprisingly patient and businesslike.

"George, there are people here!" She'd spoken in a whispered shout. She had a talent for that.

"Okay, Maureen."

He'd put the receiver down and thrown pajamas that he never used anymore into the bag. "If she calls back, Elizabeth, you can tell her about the baby if you want to. I don't care." He had cared and she'd known it. He'd also known, as she had, that Maureen wouldn't call back.

He'd zipped the bag and picked up his jacket and approached Elizabeth who had been quiet and uneasy since his fight with Tennessee.

"I don't believe you anymore, George," she'd said to him one night, *"I don't think you know what you want. You say one thing and mean another."*

"George . . ."

The color of her eyes varies. Then they were gray and troubled and he knew from the tone of her voice he didn't want to hear what might follow so he tried to head it off.

"Don't worry, Elizabeth, you know how lucky I am. I always get a seat by the toilet."

She'd smiled then, generously, letting him intervene, and he'd put his arms around her, kissing her, thinking it might be for the last time, he might be smashed into molecules in some desolate southern cotton patch or she might be carried away in the night by crazies attacking the telephone company. "Don't let any spacemen carry you away," he'd said, holding her, looking at the miraculous mixture of gold and red and brown that made up her hair. And he had been afraid to go, afraid to move, afraid to pull his arms away from her until she'd warned he would miss his plane.

Now the man with the drawn eyebrows passes down the aisle of the plane heading for the restroom, a short, slightly seedy man with graying hair, a thin body, a gray knit suit. If you bit into him he'd be gray straight through, George thinks.

It is just dark when the plane begins the descent and the city of Dallas is spread out in the distance like some jumble of bright toys tossed out of a box.

When the plane halts the passengers spill into a cavernous waiting room. It is easy to follow the gray man out of the terminal and into the warm, early night air, and then into a limousine that carries them down expressways past striking new buildings standing rawly without curbs on the flat plain. Shortly afterwards it is even easier to follow the gray man out of the limousine and into the downtown hotel.

"Elizabeth, there's a radioactive couple downstairs who claim they've been on a spaceship with creatures from outer space. Supposedly they disappeared for weeks but thought they'd only been gone a day. Something had happened to their navels."

Elizabeth does not seem intrigued. "I guess you have to see all this to believe it. Definitely not a meeting of the FCC. *Bizarre*, I think you'd say. You want a 'See you on Mars' T-shirt?"

George is looking across the small gray and orange hotel room at the picture of an old cowboy who seems odd in the middle of plastic modern.

"Have you found out anything?" she asks eagerly and he is grateful for the eagerness in her voice.

"Lost in Space isn't here yet. They're supposed to

perform tomorrow night after the banquet. So I could have waited till tomorrow. I wish I had."

He imagines her sitting at the kitchen table holding the white receiver from the wall and smoking a cigarette, dropping ashes into the Thrifty Liquor Store ashtray, probably wearing nothing under the full green African thing she wears around the apartment after work. It makes him feel lonely, makes him want to have a chance to look at her again, to put one finger on the thin line of her wrist. It makes him regret all the foolish moments he's not been brightly aware of being with her, of her breath on his cheek, her arm around his side.

"What are you doing?" he asks her.

"Nothing," she says. "Reading, watching the telly." She does them both at once, a multi-media person, a separated brain.

She told him once that she didn't like to be alone anymore. *I miss you,* she'd admitted. He is fishing for that now, but fears it will never come. Maybe because it's been said. Maybe because it isn't true any longer.

"I wish you were here," he says. "You'd love it." But his voice sounds flat, as humorless as the plastic laminated wood table beside the bed. What he wants to say is, Elizabeth, do you realize there is only a finite number of times in the rest of our lives we can make love? A limited number of times. Think of that, Elizabeth! The very thought brings me to a state of panic. Why am I here, you there? But what he says is "Dallas is interesting but the accents drive me crazy."

She says nothing and he fears she is wanting to get away, not grieving at all that he will not be there to lie beside her, to make love and kiss the soft beige skin more wonderful to him than all the outer planets or trips to Mars. For it seems to him that he's brought to her rather than happiness a great jumble of unease, a throng of worries and uncertainties. His presence maybe confuses her life which without him would be peaceful or what she wanted it to be. Now she sits peaceful amidst his jumble. And his jumble isn't even that interesting but rather a mundane, entirely pedestrian jumble. No ecstatic extremes or revolutions or planned assassinations on either side.

"You want an 'Over the rainbow is a humanoid' T-shirt?"

He can think of nothing more to say. "Did Maureen phone?"

"No," she says and he can tell by her tone that he should have asked that at the first of the conversation, not at the last.

"Well, I guess I'll go," he says. "Oh, there's a sun lamp in the bathroom. So look for a man with a tan."

She laughs lightly and says, "See you," the tone casual, it could mean if you happen to be walking down the street and I happen to be walking down the street we might meet.

"Take care, Elizabeth."

He hangs up, feeling uneasy but proud that he kept himself from discussing when he'd be back. It is altogether possible that she doesn't even want him back. The very thought of the possibility makes him feel cold and dead inside. Don't think such things, he tells himself.

He places another call and this time Grey answers. He announces himself and asks for Maureen. He catches a dramatic hesitation between the reception of the name and the summons. Then the sound is muffled and he knows Grey is warning her. It gives him a sense of power that for once Maureen will be interested in what he has to say. As he waits he takes his shoes off and pours more scotch into his water glass and lies back on the bed.

Keep control of the situation, he tells himself. Be calm. Exercise sense and restraint. Do not lash out, do not take advantage, do not perpetuate the mental cruelty you will be accused of and ruled guilty of by a court of law. He wiggles his freed black-socked toes and pokes a toe through a hole. If you could see this, Maureen, you would be ashamed, he thinks.

"Hello, George."

"I'm in Dallas, Maureen, at the space freak convention."

He can't avoid saying it, therefore reading her mind over the miles: *So it's happened, he's flipped. I hope he goes into outer space and does not pass GO and does not come back.*

"Really?" she says coolly, with the you-are-wasting-my-time-why-don't-you-fuck-off voice.

"I have discovered, Maureen, or maybe I should say . . ." Careful, George, if it's not true what a laugh, what a charge of mental cruelty could be laid against you in the great book in the sky of charges between ex-wives and ex-husbands resulting probably in eternal impotence. "Maybe I should say I have been told and am led to believe that Claudie had a baby."

She believes him immediately which is a triumph, a testimony that there is still some thread between them that allows an honest message, some space undisturbed by accusations and bitterness and failure. It is the most promising moment between them in ages.

"How do you know?"

Her voice is breathless and if Grey can hear it he is sure to drop the chapbook from Outerzoo Press and project his unadulterated, poetic concentration to what she is saying.

He tells her briefly that the friend of Claudie's he'd mentioned earlier left word that Claudie had a baby.

"What do you mean 'left word'?" she asks, suspicious now.

"Well, he was peculiar." Wrong word. She will believe it a lie, now. "He wasn't sure we should know."

"Why?"

"It's a long story, Maureen. I phoned to tell you before I left, remember?"

"Yes."

Stop, George, don't throw stones. Her voice is properly chastened.

"Anyway, it's too long and complicated to tell long distance. Just believe me when I say I think it's true and that's why I'm here, to see if I can find the baby."

"But why didn't they tell us when we were down there?"

"I don't know. They may not have known."

"Is it a boy or a girl? How old?"

"I don't know. I'll let you know everything as soon as I find out."

She doesn't speak for a minute. He hears her breathe and suddenly he can see her face clearly smiling and he feels a catch in his own throat.

"I'm going to be crazy till we know," she says.

We!

"I'll let you know as soon as I find out anything . . . What do you think?"

"It's so incredible!" She stops, overcome with the wonder of it. "But it's possible, isn't it? It's possible!"

There is such sheer, honest hope in her voice. He takes a sip of scotch and answers before he's swallowed it well.

"Yes, it's possible. Well, I better go. Goodnight, Maureen."

It was more intimate saying "Goodnight." She always said "goodbye."

But this time she said, "Goodnight," the wonder still light and high in her voice.

Claudie, Claudie. No more songs for you. The house-boat was there all right, but we were too late by miles. Wasted as the gas. Dan a box of ashes. Except we didn't believe that. We knew he was up there fiddling for the angels. Sometimes we'd hear the music, we thought.

I was gone before the baby came. Fifteen years, they gave me. Five, I figure, for stealing the hat. Not only criminal assault but smart aleck, the judge said. Never came out about the patrolman taking the Thunderbird. He claimed we hijacked him at the truck stop.

"Danny," Claudie called her. "Size of a seventy-nine-cent bag of potato chips," she wrote me. Hair like orange Jell-O. Promise me, she wrote, you'll take care of Danny if anything happens to me. Promise, she said. You are godfather without ceremony. If you have to break outta there, promise me, Tennessee.

I promised. Behind forty thousand iron bars I promised. But I was hoping the baby would make things better. And she did sometimes. But there were too many downs. And the convenient, fast ups came in smaller forms always not too far away or too hard to get. I tried to get her to leave Texas but she said she'd stay till I could leave, too. And before long the coming on film writer followed her to Austin. When she visited she always talked about Dan. About being so wrong. She'd believed that because we were young nothing was permanent, that we could always start again if we made a mistake. She said she should have known that just being alive is old, because you can die. She said she could never get used to the idea that she couldn't bring him back. She went to séances. She claimed she'd talked to him.

Sometimes she wouldn't visit. Joanne or Warren would come. From what they said the boat was sinking.

Joanne was there the last night. She asked where Claudie was. The film writer pointed to the bedroom, said she couldn't hear again. Not that he didn't care, but it was too much to deal with when you're making connections and driving cars straight through to Delaware with the threat of hot lava pouring on your head all the time.

Claudie was in the bedroom sitting on the side of the bed, her hands over her ears. It always scared her a lot when it happened. She was afraid to keep the baby alone by then 'cause a lot of time she couldn't hear. So Joanne was keeping Danny a lot. Then some new people came in with stuff right out of Mexico. Joanne took Danny home, leaving Claudie sitting on the bed.

*About three o'clock in the morning they got her to the
hospital but it was all over. I woke up that night. I
remember. Love soul premonition, Merle used to call it.*

*I told Joanne if she'd keep Danny a few months I'd be
out soon maybe with good behavior. I was in Ferguson
then. But it was looking like a few years and Joanne and
Warren . . . Well, you can't handle a toddler on a
houseboat, for Christ's sake. And Joanne was going to
school and together they couldn't make enough to feed a
chicken. I didn't know what to do. I even thought of
sending her to Merle, which shows I musta had brain fever.*

*Then one night Claudie told me in a dream to find her
father. She said he'd take care of Danny till I could. And I
said okay. But the next morning I started worrying maybe
he wouldn't really want Danny. And even if he did maybe
he wouldn't let me have anything to do with her later. I
wasn't looking for somebody who'd claim her like a
possession. And I didn't wanna be made into an enemy. So
I had to check it out.*

*When they wouldn't give me a furlough I decided to go
anyway. Some guys get away with it. So one morning I
split for D.C.*

George wakes with a circle of sunlight on his face. On
the street below people are calmly walking to work—
women in bright clothes and men in big hats making no
extraterrestrial considerations whatever.

So this is the day I might find Claudie's baby, he

thinks, recalling early marriage when Maureen would wake in the morning exclaiming, "Just think I might be pregnant!" with such pleasure, such wonder.

In the coffee shop George orders coffee and something called "Late Riser's Quickie" which sounds to him like a sex technique. In the lobby the convention is in full swing. There are booths lining the convention room and spilling into the lobby selling magazines and paperback books, extraterrestrial artifacts, privately printed tales of journeys to outer space, T-shirts, buttons, masks. For a fee he could sign up for an analysis of his psychological suitability for space travel. He could financially support a space expedition departing from a mountain in Colorado in late summer.

At ten o'clock is a meeting of the International Association for the Investigation of the Unexplained and at the same time a talk on "Why Gamma-ray Bursts?—One More Mystery Linked to Black Holes!" George chooses black holes and sits next to a heavy short-of-breath man wearing green plaid socks with part of the label still sticking to them. Occasionally he catches a familiar term. Apollo. Goddard. X-ray. Dwarf stars. Black Holes. I think I know about black holes, George thinks.

"Consider this . . ." The scientist leans forward. "Within a few milliseconds the radiation of a gamma-ray burst can start and stop. Apollo data show the radiation stopped completely for 18 milliseconds."

The man next to George takes a lengthy, difficult breath and George wonders how many milliseconds it takes to die. How long was Claudie dying? Did she know she was dying at the time? Was she terribly afraid?

"However, evidence from Helios-2 indicates the source of the gamma-ray burst protons might be only 300 kilometers—considerably smaller than the earth."

And what is the size of the earth? How many rooms of curious people? How many chairs of gasping men? How many in green socks? There is much he does not know and much he does not care to know. Why do you care? he wonders, looking at the assemblage, straining to uncover the mysteries of the universe, of gamma rays and black holes. How miraculous it seems to him that they should wonder such impossibilities and not be content to know that their own children live, that their grandchildren are safe at some known address, within the range of telephone, mail and perhaps personal communication or even the miracle of mailgrams.

In the afternoon the Astronaut Room is filled by the time George enters for the "briefing session" by Early Warning who is to lead the space expedition from a mountain in Colorado sometime in the next year. George takes a place along a wall standing beside others and waits fifteen minutes for Early Warning to appear, thinking all the while of the possibility that Tennessee might very well take Claudie's child and flee the earth with some such group of crazies.

When Early Warning enters he looks like a young lawyer except he wears a red circle pin, like his followers, the symbol of those leaving the earth. Early Warning is from Scarsdale and studied nuclear engineering at Cornell, he says, but all his life he's been looking for more. He sets forth his credentials like a political candidate only no political candidate could have had such a rapt audience. George thinks he could hear an ash drop were there one.

Early Warning is into what he calls "the process" when a couple from the audience rises and begins talking as though the floor is theirs. They are dressed pioneer style, the woman in a long fluffy dress and the man in a long beard, black pants and suspenders. They might have climbed right off a covered wagon of a TV western into the folding chairs of the Astronaut Room. It seems they not only disagree with Early Warning but have a hole in their bank account to prove the process may be another word for a very old system called "swindle." Their words are laced with a righteous fury of the disaffected.

Early Warning turns away at first and laughs uncomfortably. He tries to reply but they continue. Finally the reply becomes shouting and a rumble grows through the room slowly like an earthquake rumbling underground. The voices rise and the anger builds hotly as though it were a holy spot being desecrated by dispute. George feels the anger growing into fear and some frightening and heretofore concealed element borne off the flat Dallas plain seems to swirl into the room like snakes under the door bringing a gray whirlwind which threatens to sweep the pioneers back to the desert.

He doesn't hear what it is that starts Early Warning

toward the man with the beard. He only knows that when the move is made it is like an explosion, the room filled with those in a foreign place unaccustomed to touch in anger and perhaps in love. It is an explosion not unlike his own toward Tennessee, he thinks, fueled by frustration and fear.

There is much pushing of chairs and shouting and the man with the green plaid socks is standing on a chair shouting while a woman stands beside him crying. Then suddenly what sounds to George like a giant alarm clock goes off. It makes a strange buzzing sound like a Roman candle spinning through the air. It stops everyone in the room—Early Warning and the pioneers and the man with the socks all look around. The sound comes from a small green metal box held by a tall, thin man with diagonal eyebrows. Anticipating the attention he smiles like a magician stepping from a curtain, and bows his head slightly.

Behind George a woman says with incredulity, "It sounds just like them!"

Room 403B is across from the elevator. It would be noisy there night and day, whores and spacemen and serious scientists would pass continuously on their assorted missions. But members of the band Lost in Space would never know since their music isolates them, reverberating through the halls, their bass jolting the steel beams that support the building. George knocks on the door several times before it opens. The face appearing is familiar—heavy lips, droopy-lidded eyes and eyebrows drawn into thick carets.

George shouts that he's looking for Tennessee Blue and can he talk to them?

The kid steps back. He is wearing a tank top with a spaceship printed on it that shifts positions when he turns. His slick chest displays a gold chain with the Early Warning symbol.

Inside the room two other members of the band are lounging on chairs and drinking Ripple wine. Sitting on the bed, lined up as though for inspection, are three girls with blonde, blowsy hair. They look identical, like triplets. The music roars forth from a tape machine on the dresser. Around the tape machine are exploded packages of foil strewn with bones and a tall Colonel Sanders fried chicken carton.

One of the band members, the short stocky one with ringlets, who plays the drums, lifts a bottle of wine, offering it to George who shakes his head. The drummer turns away shrugging his shoulders as though he's been insulted. George sighs to himself thinking it is like dealing with some primitive tribe—you drink their wine and like their music or they draw swords.

George leans toward the leader's ear. "Is Tennessee still traveling with you?"

The ear leans away and the droopy eyes and the strange eyebrows turn on him suspiciously. He has refused their wine and now asks a question. Good God, George thinks, why is everyone in this country expecting to be arrested at any moment? He wants to shout questions but they wouldn't hear anyway. He glances at the three girls who are holding cigarettes now in their right hands like a chorus line. A red metal ashtray sits in the middle lap.

"Haven't seen Tennessee in several days," the leader in the tank top says. He has a way of speaking that travels through the blare. Bionic, no doubt, George thinks.

There is an insistent stomping on the ceiling which they all ignore. The leader pours himself a paper cup of Ripple wine and takes the only available chair leaving George standing in the middle like a floor show.

"You have any idea where he might be?" George shouts and mouths.

The leader shakes his head casually.

Blasé! They are all so goddamn blasé! Everyone in the world but himself. Poseurs are everywhere and what he is asking with no style at all means nothing to anyone. To hell with the rest of the hearing world. Not to mention the stranger left standing in the middle of the room!

Suddenly George has talked himself into a fury, standing there like a sideshow, while they sit drinking their goddamn Ripple wine and the three paper dolls go through their routine of ruining what is probably a perfectly good hotel mattress. For a wild, frustrated moment he considers putting his hand in his pocket and pointing it like a gun, threatening to wipe them out of the universe unless they help him. Instead in an inspired moment he crosses to the dresser and pushes the tape machine to OFF. In the stunning quiet that follows, power falls to him like magic.

"Now listen, goddamn it," he says. "I'm not the fucking CIA or the FBI. I'm looking for Tennessee for a damn good reason. It happens to be a personal reason, not official. I flew here from Washington, D.C., to talk to him. Surely it isn't going to break the space code to tell me where he is. For all I know you may all be on another planet tomorrow."

They all look sober. He didn't need a gun after all. Finally the girl in the middle smiles and he sees they are not the same. She has a thin face and eyebrows, the others have no eyebrows, only blue makeup and round faces. Whyever would he think they were the same he wonders.

"My goodness, tell him," the girl in the middle says. She has a terrible Texas accent and a pile of curls on her head but she could lead armies. George looks at her kindly.

The leader of Lost in Space lifts a chicken leg from a piece of foil. "Hey, man . . . come on. It's no big thing," he says. "You don't have to pull the Texas Rangers in here on us. I don't know where Tennessee is exactly. He left a couple of days ago heading for Austin. He was planning to stop there and head on to Mexico. He's got a friend in Austin. Sells jewelry on Guadalupe. You might check it out with him."

George pushes the tape to ON and the blare resumes. Overhead the stomping begins. Leaving he looks gratefully again at the thin-faced girl in the middle who is kicking off her green sandals.

In an hour he has deposited his space equipment and orientation packet into a wastebasket and checked out of the hotel. As he walks through the lobby Lost in Space is singing as best he can understand about being lost in the most distant galaxy. He wonders if they will sing the song about Claudie.

There are no more seats on the one plane to Austin that night so a few blocks away in a Greyhound bus station he buys a one-way ticket.

Leaving Dallas the bus crosses a thin, raggedy river and a man on a motorcycle with a brown-holstered sidearm, cowboy boots, helmet and goggles flies around the bus and into the evening. Beyond the miles of greedy suburbs the flat empty land is marked with names of people no longer there. Waxahachie, Wichita, Waco. Places where the land permitted no hiding places so that their legacy is only the words, though the highway is intersected with fortress-like overpasses resembling out-posts.

At the back of the bus young teenagers are putting dirty words to hymns. George opens the newspaper he's brought along and skims the first page for the major stories. The one international story reports the Chinese are opening beauty parlors and selling Coca-Cola. The other stories are local and soft, full of innuendo and editorializing, the old discipline of who, what, when and where in the first paragraph, gone with the Edsel. He closes the paper and stares for a while at the tall, vacant-faced female sketched on the back page in an ad. No nose, no mouth, only eyes, a sullen giant. Fleshless and languid. Fantasy, what men might think they want, what he had thought maybe once without thinking. He folds the paper and flips off the light above his head. The land and sky are dark gray, the horizon distant and barely visible. There are glimpses of small towns tucked away, their lighted gas stations making friendly lanterns in the dark. A massage parlor in a mobile home sits lighted and lonely in a field along the highway. George feels like an explorer in a strange land. In this world he has the feeling of a different space. He sees to the ends of the earth, the flat land revealing everything, giving him a strange feeling of isolation with himself.

The night becomes darker. Reflector lights loom along the highway like the eyes of great animals. For a while lightning flashes in the distance like campfires. The singing in the back wears out. An old woman across the aisle tells someone she's going to visit her daughter in San Marcos. The daughter and her husband own a barbecue place there. Proudly, she declares she's been a widow for twenty-nine years. George wonders if the pride is from having been alone so long, for having so outlived the man or for the simple fact of surviving. Any of the reasons, he decides, is worthy of celebration. Where there is nothing more to praise oneself for there is the gray heart of sheer survival.

Right? he asks himself. *Right, George,* he answers. And having had more than twenty-nine years of survival he has cause to celebrate. Indeed on this day having much more than survival—Elizabeth that moment might be passing his no longer damp bath towel, reading a magazine with his name on the address label, might even be thinking of him and a phantom child of his own blood. It is so much more than survival. And what he has with Elizabeth is based on no fantasy. Even the often painful awareness of himself and the delicacy of their relationship is good. It is alive.

And thinking this he is suddenly overwhelmed with a feeling of well-being, of more satisfaction than he has ever been conscious of, much more than when life was as he unconsciously expected it to be. Now he sees it all as rare—Elizabeth, Maureen who is happy. The child. And why the child, he asks himself, looking out the moving window of darkness. Why in a world where thousands of children die of neglect and starvation is one so precious? He thinks then of Claudie, sees her face clearly and knows it is the miracle of life that we are not interchangeable. For him the child is another chance and a reason to be grateful to Claudie, offering him another person to love when there are so few.

When the bus turns off the expressway in Austin it is near midnight and the old woman across the aisle is asleep and snoring softly. Inside the terminal a large Latin family sits with patient weariness in a row of descending heights. A tired airman sleeps in a chair and a young girl is dropping a coin repeatedly into a cigarette machine. George stops to exchange coins with the girl and listens for the solid thud of machine acceptance. The girl smiles as if it were a slot machine and she'd won, and George carries the smile along with his one-suiter into the wide main street of Austin with its quiet stone buildings that seem baked into the land. The light on the top of the state capitol glows peacefully and he thinks how far it might be seen over those flat plains, maybe all the way to Waco or to San Marcos where the old woman's daughter waits for the bus that is late.

He walks slowly down Congressional Avenue and takes a room just a few blocks away that smells faintly of fresh paint.

"Still lots of musicians around here?" George asks the man at the desk.

"Taking over the town. Young ones, old ones, all of 'em squirrelly looking."

In the tall-ceilinged room he pours himself a drink of scotch and looks out the window where a red neon sign of a Mexican restaurant flashes warmly. He looks out over the gray town toward the expressway and thinks of the small houses beyond with their front porches and short trees lower than telephone poles. Somewhere out there is Claudie's child. The child probably sleeping now and he remembers for the first time in years the special peacefulness of a child sleeping. And then, too, there is Claudie's grave. A chill passes through him, a keen, razor-edged sorrow that he will never lose. He thinks of the facts, now resting in some file, those terse, unsatisfactory words of the coroner's report. The truth had eluded those facts. The story, he has to admit, is somewhere else, maybe with Tennessee Blue. And already he feels differently, the bitterness he extended to Tennessee Blue seems to have dissipated, to have been lost along some flat gray mile.

He removes his shoes and shirt and takes a drink, then sitting on the side of the bed, lifts the receiver and dials.

There are two rings before she answers, her voice cloudy with sleep.

"Elizabeth. Hi, I'm in Austin."

"Um . . .," she murmurs sleepily.

"I just rode a bus halfway across Texas." He waits for a response but there is none. "I haven't found Tennessee but I have to talk to you." He pauses. "Elizabeth, are you awake?"

She murmurs again and yawns.

"Now listen, you do not have to say a word. Not till I'm back and not then if you don't want to."

He hears a sleepy, low, "Okay."

"Elizabeth," he begins, "first of all I want to tell you that I'm going to get a job when I get back. If I have to humble myself as well as accept austerity that's what I'm going to do. The days of wine and unemployment are ending."

"Oh," she says in a tone George takes as approval or acceptance or at least interest.

He sees out the window the red light of the Mexican restaurant flash like a stop sign.

"Now, I know it's not good timing, Elizabeth. But it may never be good timing again. You know? I may come walking in with a child to raise. Me. My responsibility, Elizabeth. And Maureen's, if she wants to share it. But we'll work that out, Elizabeth. And it will be good. I promise. And I swear to you I will never ask you or expect you to assume any role you don't want. Ever.

"See what I've learned, Elizabeth, is we can work out our problems. I'm sure." Then taking a deep breath like readying himself for a launch into an unknown, he proceeds with what he has wanted to say many times before but has been afraid to say. "And so, Elizabeth, I want you to marry me."

It sounds stilted and egotistical in some way. It's not the way he's intended it to sound.

"Whatever happens here, I *ask* you to marry me. It may not be as important as it used to be. But it's a commitment, isn't it?

"You don't have to say a word now," he adds quickly, still shocked at the revolutionary new beginning sound of it.

"Are you awake?"

"Yes, I'm awake, George," she says, softly, sleepily and as though she might be smiling.

"Well, think about it," he says. "I mean tomorrow think about it. Now go back to sleep. I'm sorry I woke you. Goodnight, Elizabeth."

"Goodnight, George."

He sets the phone down and finishes his drink. He removes his socks. There is a hole in one heel of his second and last pair of socks. He takes a quick shower and crawls between the clean, stiff sheets. Above him hangs a ceiling fan like some great dark-petaled flower. The red light from the restaurant gives the room a rosy glow. Somewhere down the street people laugh. Cars pass smoothly.

Elizabeth. He wonders if she is awake, sitting on the side of the bed smoking, looking at the glowing face of his alarm clock. Or if she is asleep already and in the morning will wonder if the call was a dream.

He smiles thinking of that and falls asleep.

The next morning is bright. George feels full of hope and change. He walks up the streets toward the pink dome of the state capitol, toward the University, down streets lined with gnarled live oaks where wildflowers grow in any stray patch of ground. He pauses near an open field to watch a class of young baton twirlers, a garden of bare legs and sparkling batons.

"*Austin,*" he will tell Elizabeth, "*is in a word, bare. Halters the size of Band-Aids. That's true, Elizabeth.*"

In a clothing store on Guadalupe the clerk wears a denim jumpsuit and brown beads that look to George like a long worm. "Can I help you?"

"I want to be invisible," George says. He looks at

himself in triplicate in the mirror. He's lost a few pounds. His face, never distinctive, is thinner. He looks closer and sees more. Something new and easier maybe.

"Elizabeth," he'll say, *"I may be different. You'll at least have to find out, won't you?"*

He leaves feeling himself transformed, black holey socks discarded, his feet breathing fresh air in ventilated moccasins handmade by mysterious Indians in Central Mexico. He strolls. His reflection in the bright windows is casual and relaxed. No palm tree anywhere. A girl with very long brown hair and a halter made of hosiery glances at him with some interest and he cannot suppress a quiet laugh. He feels buoyed, helium light.

In a while he stops at the table of a street vendor. The shadow of his wide straw hat circles the table shading the necklaces displayed on the velvet cloth. He chooses one of raw garnets for Elizabeth.

"Say, I'm looking for a friend, a musician."

The man looks up with interest and no suspicion. *No cop here,* his eyes read. George describes Tennessee and the man, not a lot younger than himself, certainly no kid, tilts his head curiously.

"Oh, yeah . . .," he says, "I've been hoping to run into you . . ."

An afternoon and an evening he waits in the outdoor beer garden behind the Armadillo World Headquarters, an enormous barnlike performance hall with murals of armies of armadillos on the wall. He drinks Shiner beer and talks to a waitress who calls herself Pinocchio. Pinocchio says she's actually a singer and is just waiting tables till she gets her all-girl rock group together. The first female rock group in Texas, she says, and absolutely revolutionary for Austin which is macho territory, gonzo, all that.

When she isn't busy Pinocchio in her Armadillo T-shirt which is not quite opaque sits at his table and tells him about her boy friend who opposes her all-girl rock group and who won't let her bring more animals home so that she feeds cats at the edge of the beer garden. They call and wait for her in the live-oak trees, their eyes glowing.

When he arrives the second afternoon Pinocchio says someone is waiting for him. It is the man who sold beads on Guadalupe. This time he shakes George's hand and says his name is Warren and that it took awhile to find out where Tennessee is.

"You're right, he sure did turn up in Austin. Got picked up getting off the bus. That's luck, isn't it! Didn't even get out the door. He's already been moved to Ellis," Warren says.

"Where's that?"

"About a hundred miles from here close to Huntsville. It's the real nutcracker of the state pen."

The electronically operated doors slide apart and George enters, passing into a hallway then to an elevator. A guard shows him into a small room and leaves. Tennessee appears. No red suspenders. Except for blue eyes it is prison white and short hair. Seeing George, Tennessee pauses for the slightest second, turns, touches his head just over his eyebrow, a nervous gesture George realizes he's seen before. The face is thinner, prison taut, the muscles in his face spooled under the tight skin. Then Tennessee moves toward him in his slow easy way, hiding whatever it is he feels. Except there is the smallest smile of the winner about his face. And George feels relieved not to have to put into words something that would not be trusted anyway.

George reaches out. They shake hands awkwardly.

"It was quite a trip. What can I say." George hears his voice too loud in the small empty room.

Tennessee shrugs. "It's okay," he says.

They sit on either side of a gray metal table, the guard watching through the window of the door, and George listens for a long while . . . San Francisco, L.A., the trip to Texas, and afterwards.

Later when the electronic doors close behind him, George walks down a flowered walk aware with every step that he has the magnificent freedom to leave the eerie silence of the machinery that is Ellis prison. He turns the rent-a-car back toward Austin, but it is miles before he escapes the fence and final guard towers. Then he watches only the sun slide down the sky and sink in the far distance beyond low blue hills. For an hour the sky is a dark blue that is not yet night.

Over the miles his mind works busily filling in blanks, answering questions, drawing a mural on the walls of his mind.

In Austin he drives to the perpetual care cemetery east of town. It is dark and the gates are locked. He drives down the road, parks the car, climbs the fence and finds Claudie's grave.

It is a light night and never has George witnessed such a depth of sky painted with such an array of stars. He wonders why in Washington when he and Elizabeth go to the top of the Washington Hotel to survey the panorama of the capital city, they mostly look down at the gray buildings along the Mall or beyond to the lighted towers in

Virginia, rarely considering the startling space above. On the rooftop gardens of the future, he proposes to himself, there'll be telescopes and lounge chairs for stargazing.

He crouches and pulls away some of the invading grass over the small square marker that is Claudie's grave. The ground is cool and hard beneath the thick clots of grass. There is a great din of surrounding night noise accompanied by the experimental songs of a mockingbird. He looks around at all the many graves and tells himself that surely there are times besides war and death when a man marks a spot and proceeds from there. Unnamed, quiet times. And so, he vows to himself and Claudie, this is such a spot and time for him. And when he leaves a bit later, walking along the grass-cushioned paths of the cemetery, where the graves are uniformly unimposing, distinguished only by an occasional plastic wreath, he feels the various threads of her short life have been woven into some pattern. And more important he sees that that pattern, that small sadly incomplete creation is not after all completely ended.

So it's all laid out now. And here I am. A long way from Mars. And Ellis is different. What they call the grown-ups' prison. No time but hard time at Ellis.

I'd been out long enough to nearly forget what it's like, not that you can, but the smell had left me. Every prison in Texas smells the same 'cause they make their own cleaning materials. But it's quieter here. Ferguson sounded like a damned zoo. Ellis sounds like the inside of an oil drum.

It ain't easy. You gotta hold your mud and move careful till people figure out how you gonna ride. It's lucky having some time behind me so I have some preparation.

But it don't take long to feel like you've been here forever, like all the past weeks outside were one long dream you had one night when you popped something that could make you sleep and dream instead of lying there rocking and rolling all night.

174

I read the letters forty times apiece and keep going over in my mind what George said. Look, you got pen pals now, *he said.* Business on the outside. Somebody checking into that patrolman. Scratching where it might hurt. Or at least look bad. *He hired a lawyer. What the fuck do I know. Maybe he will help. I wouldn't have thought he'd come here. Or go through all the tangles to bring the kid, or promise anything.*

I write a lot of letters.

Dear Merle,

I'm not making excuses. Lots of things happen you don't intend to happen. Right? I imagine you could think of some yourself. I knew I was taking a big chance leaving Ferguson. But I had to get out awhile. I had something important to do.

This is about the first time I could write. For two weeks they had me in what they call "adjustment." You can't do anything there but count your toes. Now I'm back in regular but I'm on the line, working the fields. That'll last a few months and if I'm lucky I'll get into something else. I never wanted to be a farmer.

The big thing here is the prison rodeo they have in the fall. They talk about that a lot. I told them right off I never sat a horse in my life except on a merry-go-round.

It's nice your wanting to visit but it's a long bus trip. Believe me, I know. There's nothing you could find out here I can't tell you on a page. And I don't expect to be here real long. Not as long as they think anyway. In

Ferguson I couldn't see any further than the past. Now I feel like maybe there's something ahead. I got attachments. Maybe if I ever get outta here everybody on the outside won't be strangers.

Thanks for sending the little book of prayers. You'll be surprised to hear I read them sometimes. I especially like "The Heavenly Staircase." Sounds like a song I know.

Glad to hear Robert is on the wagon. I hope it works this time.

I guess that's it for now. Take care of yourself.

Peace and music,
Tennessee

There is a red ring around her mouth from the lollipop the stewardess gave her earlier. She waves the lollipop like a wand and looks at George, her eyes as bright as the candy. Even after three weeks of seeing him regularly she is still uncertain, like him. Earlier she cried, large tears flowing steadily and he held her, making sounds he hadn't made in centuries it seemed. Finally she went to sleep.

"What will we do with one another?" he asked her sleeping face, so like Claudie's. "You think we'll work this out? You think the buffalo is extinct?"

Now she pats her feet in red sandals against his knees. Earlier in the week Tennessee told her those sandals were really *her* and she'd laughed as though she understood. When their time was up Tennessee lifted Danny high in the air, danced her to the door.

"Stay away from dark alleys," he called as he was leaving with the guard.

The stewardess stops beside them. "How you doing?" she asks Danny. "How old are you, cutie?" Danny reaches for the stewardess's extended hand and answers with an unintelligible string of words.

"Growing on one," he says.

"You her father?"

"Grandfather." The word he's not used before is a jar, as if the plane fell a few feet.

"Really! Well, lucky you."

"Yes, you wouldn't believe how lucky," George says.

Later Danny is settled on his lap, leaning against the new casual shirt, looking out the dirty window of a Capitol Cab. From National Airport he gives her a brief introduction to the city. Her eyes respond to the inflection in his voice. She watches thoughtfully.

There is dogwood—pink and white—blooming through the woods along the parkway and the green stretches along the river have a cellophane clear shine. In the city the Mall is newly planted with red and yellow tulips of plastic perfection.

"The flags hanging from the street lights are to welcome you," he tells her. The cab driver glances at him in the mirror.

On Pennsylvania Avenue a new sidewalk cafe is open and crowded, and turning onto Connecticut he sees with wonder that in his absence, after years of gaping threat, the monstrous cavern unearthed for subway construction has disappeared. Small new trees stand bravely upright. A neat "M" marks an entrance and an escalator slides down easily, proving that man has conquered the region below. It is a miracle, he thinks, this healing of his own street, reminding him that after all, things end and are completed.

In front of the apartment house he readjusts his straw hat, pays the cab driver and loads Danny in one arm with her sack of toys and a dirty stuffed doll with no hair and one eye. The cab driver carries the one-suiter and Tennessee's Venezuelan flight bag.

"Have a nice day," the cabbie says leaving.

George, having no remembrance of keys, punches buttons indiscriminately until he gets a fanfare of buzzes. As he pushes the door Danny pulls the doll closer, her eyes fearful.

"This is where I live," he says to her and pats her tiny back. "You'll like it here. Tomorrow maybe we'll go to the zoo."

He pulls the bags inside and when the door closes behind them she looks around curiously. The building feels strange to him, as though he's been to the moon and seen the earth from a great distance.